_up to 14!_

THE WIZARD
KILLER

- SEASON TWO -

BY
ADAM DREECE

ADZO Publishing Inc.

Calgary, Canada

ADZO Publishing Inc.
Calgary, Alberta, Canada
www.adzopublishing.com

Printed in Canada

This is a work of fiction. Names, characters, places, and incidents are a product of the author's imagination. Locales and public names are sometimes used for atmospheric purposes. Any resemblance to actual people, living or dead, or to businesses, companies, events, institutions, or locales is completely coincidental.

Library and Archives Canada Cataloguing in Publication
(Please contact publisher for CIP record)

1 2 3 4 5 6 7 8 9 2017-03-13 33,132

DEDICATION

To Mike, Jess, Katrina, and my other friends & fans who made me realize that I created something special. It took a while to sink in.

And to every author who is nervous about writing something different than what they're known for. Write your heart into it and jump off the proverbial cliff. When you discover you can fly, it will make you fearless.

PREVIOUSLY

In Season 1 of The Wizard Killer, we met a man with no name as he awoke from the dead with his short-sword impaled in his chest, his magic failing, and his memories scrambled.

As he ventured into the barren wasteland trying to figure out what had happened to him, he narrowly avoided being burned alive by a carn and eaten by a family of ghouls.

A chance encounter with a trio of bandits revealed he was something called a weslek, some kind of living mana-battery. Fighting alongside them in a desperate battle against two flaming carnu, the nameless man drained the remaining life force from one of the dying bandits, and shot another. The battle won, their leader, a magic-wielding woman named Ania, took off, leaving the nameless man with the haunted feeling that their business wasn't over.

And in the final moments of Season 1, the nameless man and a oner woman raced against time to escape the wrath of the raw devastation being wrought by a floating city. As the city passed over them, ripping every speck of life and mana from the surrounding area, the oner woman sacrificed herself for a chance to save the nameless man.

Welcome to *Season Two*

Soul-shredding pain, that's all there is. I can't see, I can't feel, and I can't remember how I got here. There's only wave after wave of pain, like I'm standing on a beach of torment.

In the moments between each wave, I try to think clearly, just for a second, but get knocked down and tortured for my insolence. Then it passes, and instead of appreciating the peace, I go at it again. I'm just that kind of idiot.

For the millionth time, I try, and this time, the world around me changes.

There's a grey horizon with a shining, black sun sandwiched between a flat, obsidian floor and a midnight sky.

The pain is still there, inexplicably accompanied by a buzzing, but I push them aside just in time to notice a shimmering, outlined form, some kind of giant, heading for me.

I start backing up, but the giant keeps gaining on me. Part of me wants to turn and run, but there's nothing, nowhere. I stop moving and plant my feet.

Glancing down at myself, everything's blurry. I feel around, but I can't find any weapons. I curl my hands into fists as a scowl forms on my face.

The outlined giant stops several feet in front of me and reaches out with its huge hands. Strangely, it doesn't try to grab me but grabs hold of something invisible about a foot in front of me.

The giant pulls on it, and my pain becomes blinding. Mother of Mercy, what the yig is that?

Bracing itself, the giant lifts me into the air without touching me, its hands firmly gripping something. I don't understand why I'm not blacking out from the pain.

After flailing me back and forth, it throws me down to the ground and starts encircling me.

I want to cough, but there's no air. Curious, I reach out in front of me, but I can't feel whatever the giant was holding on to.

Where I am, it doesn't have the same rules as everything else. Concentrating, I feel something at the back of my mind: something important.

I stare at the black sun. It's almost like it's calling to me.

Out of the corner of my eye, I see the giant's getting ready for another approach, its hands out in front, ready to grab the invisible object again.

Suddenly I'm wracked by something sharp and strange out of nowhere. I instinctively cover my ears with my hands. It's painful, drilling into my thoughts.

The giant turns. Its hands move back and forth... There's something else... someone else? Why can't I see them?

That thing, the strange thing... it's got less bite. It's almost melodic. It's... sound.

The giant throws its hands up. It's annoyed.

My eyes dart about as I think, the buzzing trying to distract me and failing. That's got to be a voice.

Raising my chin, I point at the giant. "I don't know how, but I'm certain that you and that sun are my ticket out of here."

The giant grabs the space in front of me again and pulls. I'm yanked off my feet like a doll and tossed about. The pain's intense, but I don't care.

As I focus on the giant, its shape and features become more clearer. Then it says something... no, yells something. It's frustrated. The giant lets go and looks over in the same direction as the last time. Squinting, I can make out the outline of someone else.

I turn my attention to the giant just in time to see it nod and march on over.

Staying still, I wait to see what it's got in mind.

It puts one hand on the invisible object, and it goes to put the other one on my shoulder.

You're going to touch me? Big mistake. I grab its hand and everything vanishes in a bright flash.

Red. Why's everything red? A shadow appears in the red, and I flinch, opening my eyes a crack. The brutal sun of the real world rages in.

My body feels like I've been trampled by a hundred horses, with a distinct pain in my chest. Also along for the ride, my stomach's upside down and that incessant buzzing is still there.

The world's a blur, but I can make out someone's got their hand on the short sword that's in my chest and I've weakly grabbed their hand.

It takes me a few blinks to focus, but I can finally see them properly. They're wearing a beige long coat, open and with the collar up, past their ears. A big pair of goggles occupies most of their face, the rest's taken up with a triangular silvery-metal and brown-leather thing over their mouth. Under the coat, they've got a long-sleeved, dirty shirt and brown pants.

They yank their hand away from mine and yell something that I'm sure's a swear. I let my arm fall limply to the ground and shut my eyes.

I listen intently as they get into an argument with someone else. The one in front of me's a woman; the other one's a guy. Huh, my mind must have imagined her as the giant. But what was she grabbing?

Peeking out, I see that they're arguing, but she's definitely the tough of the duo. Glancing down I see what the yig she was grabbing. My short sword's impaled in my chest, right where the oner woman put it.

I roll my head a bit back and forth, remembering for a moment what happened. I'm tempted to feel my wrists, but I'm pretty sure that I don't have a vine, or anything this time, to tell me how long I've been dead. And given that the scavengers aren't dead, it means the oner woman's either dead or gone.

The more the duo talk, the more it starts to make sense to me, until I realize that they've been offered money for something and need to get the job done. I'm willing to bet the job's something to do with me— why else would they still be here?

The pain in my chest's getting worse. Right. I've got to get that thing out of me, or I'm going to die for real or be suspended again. I need to think of something.

"He's awake!" shrieks the guy salvager. He's dressed pretty much the same as the woman.

I snap my eyes open and point right at the guy. "Get this yigging thing out of me."

He screams like a little girl, and I lower my hand. Wow, just pointing took everything out of me. This isn't good.

I try to draw a breath, but it hurts too much. This is going to get really bad, really quickly. My stomach's feeling oddly calm. Does that mean there's magic or not? All I know is that I'm feeling dizzy.

"How is this possible?" says the woman salvager. "The stone man can't be alive!"

Summoning everything I've got, I reach up and try pushing against the hilt. "Come on," I grunt through clenched teeth. "Get this out of me."

They grab on, and after a few tugs, it comes out.

They drop the sword, astonished.

With a hand over my bleeding chest wound, I force myself onto my side and crawl over to it.

I grab the sword and run my thumb along the etched markings at the base of the blade. A small wave of warmth trickles into me and stops. Looking down, I've stopped bleeding but still feel like complete crap.

I miss something that the woman scavenger says but catch a glimpse of her rushing towards me. She lands a solid kick in my ribs that drops me to the sandy ground. Stamping on my hand forces me to let go of the short sword. Out of the corner of my eye, I see her take off with it.

Coughing, I roll onto my side. The guy's picking stuff out of the sand from where I'd been lying. He tosses one in the air and catches it.

The charging crystals I was laying on. I remember now, the wesleks chained to the bottom of the floating side. They were ripping the life essence and mana out of everything and then they felt me… and rebelled. Instead of feeding the demonic machines that kept the city afloat, they pulled everything from it.

Blinking about slowly, I roll over and see the scavengers taking off with their hand cart.

I lose consciousness for a while. When I awaken, I'm surprised that there's nothing eating my leg or something.

Sitting up, I groan as my ribs remind me that I'm very much in the real world.

Yig, they've got my short sword. Frowning, I remember how it barely had anything to heal me.

Getting my weary ass up, I stumble over to where the guy scavenger had found the charging crystals. I kneel down in the sand and dig, finding several more. All of them are dull.

"These are dead. Is this why I'm still alive? Wait, that means that this is where the barn was."

I take a moment to look around. There's nothing. No fields, no buildings, not even a sign of the scavengers. Just white sand, and a thin plume of smoke rising in the west. I'm willing to bet that's where they went.

Glancing about, there's no sign of the oner woman

or Randmon. Rubbing my wrist, I shake my head. I could have been here for days, weeks, even years. The oner couldn't have easily moved me either, as the suspend-life enchantment would have turned me to white stone.

"Assuming I was laying there the whole time and that no one tried to move me, that means it's got to be here somewhere... unless some yigging scavenger found it."

I dig until my fingertips start to bleed, and then push a bit further. My persistence is rewarded as I hit something.

A laugh escapes me. "Come on. I can't believe that you'd leave me."

After a bit more work, I pull out something wrapped in a cloth that makes my face fall. "The oner had that..." I unwrap the treasure and stare at my mana-pistol.

A smile cracks my dry lips as I slip my hand around the grip. "Glad you don't hold a charge, or you'd be useful."

I run my hand along its flat sides and stare at the blue streak that runs from the bottom of the handle through to the end of the barrel.

"I'm in the mood for getting back what's mine and dishing out some pain. You in? Good."

Reaching the top of a sand dune, I finally see the end of the eternal, white beach. About a hundred yards away, it changes to burnt, brown land but with a road. This feels more familiar; road's always good.

Putting my hands over my eyes to shield them from the sun, I spot a few big tents a ways down the road. They look like the type you'd set up and stay in for a few weeks.

Squinting at the landscape, I shake my head. The tents are colored; one looks blue and another red. Who the yig wants to put up a sign that says 'Hey, come over here'?

I snap my fingers. Traders would. Making my way to the road, another thought hits me. Bandits would, too: Hey sucker, come over here and give us your goods.

Hmm. Still, it's a bit of civilization. Rolling my aching shoulders, I grunt. If I walk away from this with some information, goods, or a bloody workout, I'll consider it a win.

Rubbing my parched throat, I squint up at the sun. "Mind not killing me off just yet? I've got some things I'd like to do."

Nothing.

The sun's a brutal friend and a worse enemy.

As I walk, the heat mirages keep messing with me, making me think I've found water. You're a real kinpak, sun, you know that?

I stop, my eyes shifting about. Kinpak? I scratch my cheek and look around, as if I'd find someone whispering words into my ear, but there's nothing. Maybe I'm just going crazy. That'd be a relief.

My body's hurting from head to toe as the last of the effects from the short sword's magic wear off. Thankfully the scavengers didn't know how to give a real beating, as my ribs aren't as bad as they could have been. Though, knowing my luck, someone's going to make up for the scavengers' shortcomings. Maybe I should shoot everyone I come across, just to be safe. Glancing at my pistol, I'm sure it agrees.

As I make my way, the wind picks up every now and then, throwing dust in my face. Several times I stop, certain I've heard something, but all I've got are the lonely, rolling hills staring back at me and a plume of smoke further ahead, westward.

I finally get close enough to make out that there are three tents, their flaps rippling in the wind. They look a bit worn from here. Maybe they've been here a while.

The blue one's the smallest of the three, the dark red one's next, and then there's a large beige on on the far side. They're setup in a crescent, probably with a fire pit in the middle.

As I walk up, a shiver runs through me and my attention is stolen by the tent flaps. They're oddly shaped, uneven... actually, they only go a few feet up and, come to think of it, there's too many of them. A decent tent has one or two if they've got an open side, these... it's more like something ripped through the walls.

I straighten up and scan about, renewing my grip on my mana-pistol. If there were traders alive, they'd have sewn it up. It's bad for business to look like you're poor or desperate, or worse, been raided.

Taking a deep breath, I rub the stubble around my mouth. So what's going on?

Checking that nothing's behind me, I keep going.

As I cautiously approach, my eyes are drawn to dark spots around the torn flaps of the blue tent. About twenty feet out, it clicks in my head: They're blood stains. Looking over, the red tent's got them too.

Can't I find a place where people attack me with beer? There better not be ghouls here. I yigging hate ghouls.

I take a deep breath and try to feel around inside me. My chest feels normal, almost numb. I don't know if that means I have some mana stored up or not. I guess there's only one way to find out.

My face twitches a few times as the buzzing in my head increases. I shove it aside, hard.

Stalking around the blue tent, I can't see anything under the tent flaps or between the spaces. My heart's beating fast. The thought that keeps going through my head is that I don't have my short sword, and that means no healing, and no healing means the real possibility of ending up dead-dead.

Stopping at the edge of the tent, I study the flaps again for a moment. If I didn't know better, I'd think something had been cutting through them from the inside, and that something couldn't reach higher than about four feet. Wish I could tell how long ago whatever happened, happened; but nothing's giving me any hints.

I spin around, certain I heard something. Scowling, I slowly scan the landscape and listen. At first, there's nothing, but then I hear a faint, repeating, clicking sound. It reminds me of what I heard earlier, except this is stronger. I swear it's making my teeth hurt.

My pistol at the ready, I peek around the side of the tent. There's a fourth one setup to enclose the center. It's another beige one, and has a completely open front. The back's ripped into strips like the others.

Turning to the gaze upon the center of the camp, my blood runs cold.

There's an ox or cow carcass that's been ripped in half, its ribs exposed, and flies are everywhere. Around it are pieces of about a dozen people: a skull here, part of a spine there. The fire pit itself looks a small army ran through it.

Judging by the swarm of flies, I'm thinking this is fairly recent. A few days, maybe?

The clicking sound picks up. This time it makes me break out into sweat, with a stream starting to run down the middle of my back. The pistol feels slippery in my hands.

Narrowing my eyes, I take a more careful look at everything. The bodies are all over the place. There are some hatchets and broken rifles lying about, a few pistols too. There's some bedding and two travel trunks that look untouched over in the big beige tent.

A glint of sunlight catches my eye. I can't believe it. The oner woman's serrated blades are lying haphazardly on the ground in front of a travel trunk. These guys were either thieves or traders. Maybe those scavengers had already been by once before.

The buzzing in my head becomes a violent

pounding, and I stumble to the ground. I drop my pistol and put my hands on either side of my head, pushing hard. I swear my head's going to split like a ripe melon any second.

"Get up. This would be a stupid way to die," I grumble through clenched teeth. Tearing a hand away from my temple, I pick up my gun and stand up.

Out of the corner of my eye, I think I see something, but when I turn, there's nothing. This is driving me crazy.

With my pistol arm outstretched and braced by my other hand, I make my way around the campsite. Turning, I notice something weird and go back. Staring intently, I swear I'm looking through a flawed glass window, but there's no window. Moving about so that the trunks are on the other side, I'm certain that something's going on because they don't look right.

The chattering sound changes, and two words escape from my scrambled memories and leap out of my mouth: "Wind spiders."

My hands start to tremble as I feel the eyes of predators on me. What the yig's a wind spider? Come on brain, tell me!

My ears are filled with that unmistakable sound of hollow bone hitting hollow bone really fast. Then it's gone all of a sudden. I try to swallow my panic, but it gets stuck in my throat.

I bend down and pick up a piece of broken sword. Creeping around carefully, I find another area that doesn't look right and throw the sword at it. The yigging thing moves, and the clicking sound starts again from the new spot.

Running a hand over my sweaty head, I take a steadying breath. I'm not liking this at all. I freaking hate ghouls, but I love them compared to spiders. Freaking kinpak mother—

"Where's that word coming from?" I yell, immediately feeling like the king of all idiots as something hits me square in the chest. I hit the ground hard, the wind knocked out of me. My pistol flies out of my hands.

There's something moving back and forth a few yards from me... no, there's two. I glance about. Yeah, there's more.

The clicking sound fades, but once again, I can feel it in my bones.

My pistol's sitting a few feet in front of me, between me and them. There's a good chance I can get to it before I'm dead but zero chance I'd get to use it without being smart about it. I don't like those odds. Peeking over my shoulder, I see the two trunks and think of the oner's serrated swords. I crawl backwards until I hit one of the two trunks.

The buzzing in my head steps up a level, making it hard to concentrate on what I'm seeing, let alone thinking. My eyes are the thinnest of slits as the world's becoming agony to take in.

Inching my fingers back, I grab one of the swords. Everything starts going black. I feel myself grabbing the hot steel of the other blade and standing up as I black out.

What's going on?

episode three

"Hey!" yells a deep voice, followed by a hard shove.

I stumble backwards, disoriented, knocking over the chair I must have been in. I hit the wall and slump down. My head feels two sizes too small. Where am I? Why's my heart racing?

The smell of stale and rancid beer immediately assaults my nose, clearing some of the fog in my mind and waking me up.

Looking down at what's on my hands, I'm distracted by the floor's shiny, orange-and-brown sheen. Half my brain tells me the stuff on my hands feels like sandpaper; the other half, like dried snot.

My eyes go from the floor to my sleeve, and then to how I'm dressed. I'm wearing matching brown pants, vest, and long coat—all neatly pressed. On the uneven table in front of me sits a brown, bowl-shaped hat.

After a momentary debate of whether to rub my eyes, I decide against it and gaze about the rest of the bar, ignoring the figure standing beside me.

The tavern has 'rock bottom' written all over it. The dingy walls and bowing ceiling don't do it any favors. There are a few high windows, though I suspect they've never been cleaned, and thankfully they're keeping most of the morning light at bay.

The man standing beside me goes to flick my ear, and I slap his hand, glaring at him.

He clears his throat and glares back at me. He's got a tall, stocky frame and a big, bushy beard that is dark brown with a white streak from lip to chin. In one of his meaty hands is a black bowl hat, his wiry hair showing that he's been wearing it for a good part of the day already.

Under his dark long coat is a red-and-silver vest with the chain of a pocket watch showing. Most importantly, he's got a two-bar, tin rectangle pinned on the outside of his coat and the scowl of authority to accompany it.

"Sheriff," I say grudgingly.

His face relaxes a touch. "I've had to look all over town for you. You've almost missed your time to meet with the librarian, and if you miss this one, there ain't going to be another. Now get up and get moving. She doesn't stay in one place long. And if a Scourge patrol finds her? You're going to be looking over both shoulders every minute of every day until you're having a dirt nap."

I put a hand out.

He reluctantly grabs it and hauls me to my feet. My head's throbbing, and the empty beer mugs on the table tell me why. Rolling my other shoulder, it barks at me painfully.

"Mother of Mercy," I say under my breath. I must have done something to it when I fell off my chair… or last night. All that remains of what happened is a vague hint, nothing more. I can't remember walking into this place or drinking a thing. All the consequences and none of the fun, that's no way to live.

"I know that look," he grumbles, a disapproving smirk on his face. "When you strolled into town yesterday, I told you to stay away from the black beer. That stuff will knock the smile off a horse. I also told you not to play cards with the three sisters who run the place. From what I heard this morning, you're lucky they left you with your dignity, never mind your clothes."

I grimace as the shoulder pain subsides a bit. "I'll keep that in mind."

"Good. Now put some gloves on," he says pointing at my bare hands.

I pull my sleeves up and stare at my arms. "Where are my tattoos?"

The sheriff raises an eyebrow. "I was talking about your hands." He takes one of my hands and turns it sideways. There's a blue line that runs along the edge, disappearing up my sleeve. I look at my other hand, it's there too.

"Unlike most folk, I don't care where you came from, and I care even less what horrible things happened to you to put that on you. I'm sure it's why the librarian will meet with you, but I don't want to know."

He bends down and picks up a pair of gloves from under the table. "Put these on." He then hands me my hat. "Keep your head down, and no one should notice the line at your neck." He leans in. "You remember that much, don't you?"

I nod and put the gloves and hat on.

"You all good?"

"Yeah," I reply.

We step out of the bar and into the blinding, dusty outdoors. The sky's got a familiar red haze to it. My fingers start rubbing together like they're pulling on a fishing line with an unwilling memory on the end of it.

There's about two dozen people walking about, all of them dressed up beyond what I'd expect for an outskirts town. Most of the women have shiny dresses and parasols, and most of the men long coats and hats. Either this place is rich in something, or it's got a secret that some pay handsomely for.

Glancing about at the two-storey buildings and dirt-road nature of the town, knots start to form in my stomach. I'm not sure if I'm paranoid, or I remember something, but I've got a bad feeling about the place.

I nudge the sheriff and point at the red haze. "What's that?"

He gives me a wide-eyed glare. "You stupid or something?"

I frown at him.

Leaning in, he whispers. "It ain't smart to bring up the affairs of wizards and the like."

I'm tempted to ask something else, but am interrupted by the image of a floating city being built. Mana leaks... it's one of the things that can lead to this haze, I remember. Looking again, my stomach turns as I'm sure there's something far worse going on than building a floating city.

"Come on, people'll start staring," he says, leading the way.

I keep my head tilted down as people walk by. "They're building that pretty close to a town, aren't they? I thought they were always paranoid about that type of thing."

He gives me a sharp glare and gets right in my face, his hand resting atop the pistol on his hip. "I believe in upsetting the apple cart a bit every now and then. That's why I'm helping you. There are things most unnatural happening, and they've got to stop. But I need you to understand; I ain't going to risk my life or this town."

I slowly nod. Everyone likes to be a little bit of a rebel.

"Wizards have eyes and ears everywhere. I've heard a man mention a certain one, and then out of nowhere appears a hot-headed acolyte with the powers of a god and trigger-happy soldiers with something to prove." He pulls back and straightens his vest. "Now, shut up or I'll shoot you. We clear?" He flashes a politician's smile and starts moving.

Across the street's a two-storey building with a sign reading *General Store*. There's an old man, bald, staring at me.

I stare back. There's something about him, like he's a person standing among paintings, something that makes him more real than the rest.

Taking a step into the road, the sheriff immediately gets in front of me and shoves me back. "I think we're having a communication problem."

I point at the general store, but there's no one there. "I thought I saw someone I know."

"Doubt it," he replies with a scoff.

I look first at the store's door, which doesn't look

like it's closing, and then around, but there's no sign of him. The only thing out of place is a faint buzzing in my head. Strange. I can remember every detail of the man's face. I swear I've seen him before... just not here.

Shaking it off, I follow the sheriff for a few blocks before tapping him on the shoulder.

He turns around, his face showing his frustration.

I raise a finger. "Do you hear that? There's like— a clicking."

He listens for a moment. "Might be coming from the trailer house," he says gesturing at a long building coming up. "That's where we have the levi-cars. A few horses, too. Sometimes those levis make funny noises when people are working on them."

As we continue walking, I keep glancing about, unable to shake the feeling of being watched.

I perch my sweaty hands on my belt, feel something. Looking down, I see I've got an empty holster on one side. On the other, I've got an empty place for a knife. Yig, maybe there was something to that three sisters thing.

Finally, he stops and turns around, leaning towards the light-blue door of the white-washed two-storey building. Glancing around the main street, I'm sure that clicking sound is not coming from the levi's place.

The sheriff takes his hat off and taps twice on the door with his knuckles. He listens for a second, then straightens up and puts his hat back on. "Go on in. You've got five minutes, and then you need to get out of here."

I narrow my eyes at him, tempted to ask why.

He rolls his shoulders and scans the street, his hands resting on his pistols. Glancing at me, he's got an anxious look in his eye. "Go on. Clock's ticking."

I start to push on the door and stop. "You hear it too, don't you? It's like... like hollow bone being hit on hollow bone."

"Doesn't matter. Scourge spies are going to know something's up soon and I'm not going to have this town known as the place where the only free librarian died."

My palms are sweaty, my heart's racing. Something bad is about to happen. I just don't know what.

The sunlight from the door stops two feet into the room with no rhyme nor reason. Stepping into the room, I close the door and take my hat off.

I stand quietly, listening to the creak of the floorboards under me, waiting for my eyes to adjust. The room seems barren, except for a counter a few feet away.

"Gah… that sound." I put a finger in my ear and give it a good shake.

A silhouette appears behind the empty counter. "These are dangerous times," it says, the voice soft and melodic.

The head turns and I'm thrown off. It's like staring at a star-filled night sky.

Swallowing nervously, I nod. "You're the last of the free librarians I take it."

There's a scream outside, followed by another.

My hands twist my hat, and I stare at the door. "I'm…" I turn and face the librarian. "I'm told you'll have an answer for me. Though, I hate to say it, I wasn't told what the question was."

"The answer is a yes. A wizard can be killed through means other than simply time and frailty of the body. There's a High Acolyte who knows... in Banareal. He's learned the secret experiments of his master, the Wizard of Banareal. The Wizard suspects him of treachery. It won't be long before the High Acolyte is arrested and tortured."

"Are we supposed to get him before he's arrested? After?" I don't even know what I'm talking about. Staring at the floor, an image comes to me. "Old man. Is he an old man?"

I can feel her staring at me; I've thrown her off.

"The High Acolyte will be alive for some time, though barely. The Wizard will experiment on him, to see if it's possible to make an acolyte into a weslek."

"So, we need to get him out?"

"The wards won't allow him to leave the laboratory alive."

I glare at the librarian. "How is this helpful?"

Several gunshots go off on the other side of the door. It's followed by screeches and a wave of that bone-chattering sound.

"I must go," says the librarian, pushing open a door at the back, the room filling with sunlight.

Wincing and turning away, I raise a hand. "If I

follow what you're saying, then we need to get him out of there. How do we do that?"

"Take his life from him then give it back. There are a few who can craft such magical weapons. You'll need to be careful, and make it discreet."

"Like one of the soldiers' short swords?"

I wish she had an expression; I can't tell if she's agreeing or staring me like an idiot.

"We are out of time." She exits and the back door closes, leaving me standing in the dark.

The screams outnumber the gunshots. There's that clicking sound coming from everywhere, even above me somewhere.

I crack the door open a bit and look. The scene doesn't make sense, people shooting at nothing and being ripped apart by nothing.

Without thinking, my hand goes into one of the long coat pockets and pulls out an orb. It's maroon and sleek-looking, with a silver streak. Holding it up to my mouth, I mutter some words without thinking. The orb pulses.

"It's the H. A. of Banareal that we need. He's going to be taken soon, we have a limited window of time. Wards will stop us from taking him, so we need to suspend his life. We need to find someone who can put that kind of enchantment on a common item, like a short sword. Suspend his life; then we get him out of there."

Leaning against the doorframe, sweat drips off my forehead. Bowing my head for a second, I recall someone warning me that the orb could suck the life out of you, but wow, I wasn't ready for this. I feel like I've got the flu of the century.

I stroke the silver streak of the orb. It pulses once, and it's done. I stuff it back in my pocket.

Alright, now I've got to get out of here.

Pulling the door open fully, I take in the gruesome scene. There are pieces of bodies everywhere.

Across the street, I see terrified people huddled together on the second-floor balcony. If this was a Scourge Patrol, they wouldn't be safe up there, and I've known Scourge Patrols to be brutal but never to rip people apart like what I'm seeing.

I'm not taking any chances. I step out of the building, closing the door behind me. Glancing each way, I don't see any fighting going on.

I give the orb a squeeze and toss it into the air. It falls, like a lump, to the ground.

I shuffle over and scoop it up. "Come on, you're supposed to go." Tossing it again, I glare angrily as it lands without dignity on the brown, dusty, main street.

Picking it up and shaking my head, I notice the sheriff's body, one of his arms missing. A thought slips out from my foggy memories and I look around. "Whatever they're doing that's causing the red haze, there's not enough mana in the air to activate the magic for the orb." I glare at the ground. "What was I supposed to do?"

As if replying, the sheriff gives me the answer. "It needs more from me."

Just then I catch sight of a blur in the wind, then two more. This isn't what I needed.

I reach down and snatch one of sheriff's long-barreled pistols. Spinning the chamber with the back of my hand, I see its got three hopes of me living loaded. It's not much, but it might be enough to get me to more.

Scanning about, I notice that only the door to the general store is closed. Maybe people are holed up in there, or maybe it's a front for something. Either way, it strikes me as a good place to go.

I make a dash for it, the clicking bone on bone sound erupting from everywhere. The people on the balcony start screaming and crying. They've probably watched and heard this play out a dozen times already; now they're waiting for my torturous end. I hope to disappoint them.

Peeking over my shoulder, everything's deformed and distorted, like I'm looking through warped glass.

"The wind spiders are all around you!" yells a

woman from the balcony.

I've never heard of wind spiders.

Sliding to a stop in front of the general store, I turn and accidentally shoot blindly. Yig, down to two.

Holding the orb tightly up to my chest, I wait, my heart pounding. It feels like each thought of mine is fighting through a raging river to get heard, and the river's growing.

My eyes dart about, waiting for the inevitable. Everything's quiet.

I scream as something slashes my leg. Falling to the ground, I drop my pistol and put a hand over the bleeding wound. It's like someone's put warped mirrors all around me, making the whole world look weird.

I rub my blood hand on the orb. "That's got to count for something," I mutter.

The orb pulses twice as I get slashed again, this time from the left and right.

I feebly lob the orb into the air. My heart sinks as nothing happens, as it falls towards the ground. But then it turns, arcing up, and vanishes.

With renewed vigor, I grab the pistol and scramble backwards to the general store's door. I bang on the door with one hand, and fire at a warped area. Nothing on either front.

I crane my head, looking up at the door, and bang

hard again. Then I gasp, as something pierces my chest, pinning me to the door.

All I can get are short, shallow breaths. There's blood seeping out of me.

Glancing about, I see there's a slight purple in the air. Then I see it, in all its terrifying glory: the wind spider. It smells of death, and radiates sweaty heat.

I plunge the pistol into where I figure its mouth is and pull the trigger.

Yellow goo goes everywhere, and the other blurry images back off, at least for a moment.

The pistol tumbles out of my hand as it goes numb. I can't breathe. My head hurts.

I close my eyes, waiting for the inevitable.

———————

Forcing my eyes open, I'm standing in the middle of the campsite, holding the black, serrated swords. There's yellow ichor and translucent purple pieces of wind spider all over the place. The tents are even more shredded than before.

"What the? What happened here?"

I can feel my heart calming down. Tilting my head to the side and closing my eyes, I can't find the buzzing. It's gone.

Staring at the swords and then at my arms, and then the rest of my body, I see I'm covered in the yellow wind spider blood and pieces of gunk that I don't even want to think about. The only wounds I can find on myself are light cuts and scratches.

"Wait, I did this? Those things haven't been dead long, they're barely translucent!"

Squinting at the campsite battlefield, I pick out about a half-dozen or so see-through purple carcasses of wind spiders.

"Yig me."

Something twitches beside me.

I let out a soul-curdling yell and drive both blades through it hard.

Breathing heavy, my eyes wide, I wait.

The wind spider leg doesn't move.

I take a step back, ready for it. But nothing happens.

Then a laugh escapes. "Yeah, really scary. A swarm of wind spiders, you do it in your sleep. But a twitchy dead one? That one you go full barbarian on."

I scrape some of the muck off my face and dust off my hands. Rolling my shoulders and straightening up, I grimace as my muscles inform me that the battle did have some cost.

Grabbing hold of one of the swords, I wiggle it back and forth until it finally comes out of the wind spider carcass.

Scanning about to make sure no one's waiting for their moment to strike, I wiggle the other one loose.

A heavy sigh escapes as all my adrenaline leaves, and I feel just how exhausted my body is.

I drag my sorry self over to the two travel trunks. Dropping down, I lean my head against a trunk and close my eyes for a minute.

I stagger backwards and open my eyes, squinting. Looking about, I find I'm standing in the blue tent. The oner's swords are in my hands, dripping yellow goo. That yellow stuff's all over the place, along with chunks of things going purple again. What happened here?

Wiping my face with my forearm, I draw a big breath and try to think. Not surprisingly, my head's a foggy mess but I don't give up.

I remember blacking out by the trunks... but standing as that happened. Glancing down again, I confirm that I am indeed holding the swords.

But there... there was a red thing... wasn't there? Maybe it was a weird dream. And since when did I start sleepwalking, never mind sleep-killing invisible monsters?

I get a good grip on the handles of the serrated blades and wait for something to happen, but nothing does. Glancing up at the late afternoon sun, I decide it's time to check out the trunks.

Twice I trip on something and jump, expecting it to attack, but instead I notice yellow oozing out of it. Did I really do all of this?

I put the swords down and pick up my mana-pistol, tucking it into the back of my pants.

With a quick look around to satisfy my paranoia, I give the first travel trunk a shove. It's got a good heft to it.

The second trunk rocks too easily. Pulling out my pistol, I peer around it. I see that one of its dark wooden sides has been broken through. That must have been where its lock was.

Was someone trying to get in, or was something trying to get out? A shiver runs down my spine.

Hmm... a thought occurs to me, and I flip the switch on the bottom of my pistol then open the handle. "Three standard bullets."

I narrow my eyes. "I already knew that, didn't I?" I close it back up and flip it back to working off my mana.

I crack my neck and fingers. "Time to give up your secrets," I say to the trunks.

Bouncing around first, to try and get some adrenaline flowing, I wind up and give the light trunk a solid kick, sending it end over end.

"Come on!" I yell at it, my pistol pointed and ready. Creeping around to the broken opening, I peer in from a yard away.

Putting my pistol on the ground, I grab hold of the trunk with one hand and lift it up so the sun shines on it. There's a shiny cup and plate and a small roll of blue fabric at the far end. That's it. No monsters or severed heads. I'm almost disappointed.

Turning to the other one, my eyes focus on its sturdy looking lock. "Oh, think you're a challenge, do you?"

I whack it hard with the hilt of the sword.

"Yig me!" I yell, dropping the sword and massaging my hand. "Mother of Mercy that's some nasty vibration."

Giving the lock a closer look, I'm certain it's not magical like the trunk I'd found once before. But still, that was pretty stupid of me not to check. I must still be all hopped up on excitement from all this killing I don't remember doing. I need to calm down and think more. If there had been a magical trap on this, it could have blown me to pieces.

After considering a few different ideas, I shake my head as I come back to the only one that's likely to work.

I pick up the sword and give the lock another solid whack. A third hit breaks a piece of it off that nearly takes out my eye, but the lock's done.

"Nice try at a counter attack there. Better luck next

life."

I make my way to the side of the trunk and open it. If there's a conventional trap, I don't want to get shot in the face or hit by poison darts in the throat or something.

The trunk opens without a problem. On the top are rolls of red, blue, and green silks. I try to find a cleaner part of my hand, and run a finger along the silks. "That stuff's worth some good coin."

I bring the other trunk over and lay the silks on it, then I dive back in.

"Huh, thank goodness for small miracles." I pull out some decent looking clothing: shirts, vests, pants, even boots.

So, these people were traders. That's some serious bad luck to run across wind spiders. The traders either didn't know this area had them, or there's some mana leakage going on that's drawing them in.

My eyes dart around as I try to find where that memory came from. The only other thing coming to mind is that they turn a shade of purple when they die, but I already figured that much out.

I lay out a set of clothes and boots that look like they'll fit and keep digging around in the trunk.

Hauling out a small brown bag, I open it up and laugh as I pull out a six-inch-long wooden handle. Pushing on the end, a beautiful razor comes out of the handle.

"Oh wow." Holding the blade up close, I can't see a lick of rust on it. Unbelievable.

I squint up at the sky. "Doesn't look like anything's about to fall on me, and the hair on the back of my neck's not standing up. So, does this mean I could have a shave? Or as soon as I put my weapons down to do that, are wind spiders or other yigging nightmare garbage going to show up?" I put it back in the bag and put it aside.

"I know my luck. Although…" I go to tug on my unruly beard and realize it's not there: there's just stubble. My hand's drawn to my head, where I find that my hair's gone. Like my face, it's stubble.

But last time I came back to life, I still had hair, didn't I? Maybe it was the thing with the wesleks. Huh.

Now I'm feeling something off. I pick up the swords and lay them right at my feet and tuck my pistol into my pants again.

After yet another suspicious scan of the campsite, I reach into the trunk. Treasure.

"Mother of Mercy, seriously?"

It's a leather bladder full with some liquid. I undo the top and smell it, nothing. I hold it up, dripping some in my mouth. Water, it's definitely water. I can't believe it. I take a quick gulp and put it aside. Lastly, I find a full loaf of bread wrapped in a thin towel.

I plunk myself down and lean against trunk. Gazing upon the carnage and ruin around me, I eat and drink. I'm a king of a desolate land.

As the sun starts to set, I tie up the water bladder. Night's coming, and I need a plan that's better than just 'head west towards the smoke and see what happens during the night.' I'm pretty sure that if that carn that hated me so much didn't die, it'll find me. And though I'm confident wind spiders don't come out after dusk, there's a thousand other things I don't want to run into in pitch black.

Sighing, I force my weary self up. "I need to figure out how I can stay here."

Hmm. I realize I haven't done a thorough search of the whole area, so I get on it. I turn up four empty pistols and a belt pouch of bullets. While the pistols are old and cheap looking, the bullets are better. A few of them fit my mana-pistol. It's not bad to be topped up.

Finding two scabbards large enough for the oner's swords, I cut up a leather vest from one of the dead guys for straps. It's a good fit; I should be able to run with the swords on my back if I need to. Ha, if.

I look at the smoke that's been coming from the west and wonder how far away it is. I'm tempted to just go for broke. I've got a full stomach and enough water for at least two days. And then the argument to end all arguments pops up, as I remember that I don't have my short sword. Yigging scavengers, I'm going to enjoy running into them again.

I'm tempted to make a fire, but my head's telling me that the last thing I should do. Anything with a curious soul will come for miles.

Folding my arms, I stare at the too familiar campsite. "So, what do I do, just lay down among the blood and guts?" I shake my head. "Sleeping on the ground and out in the open's a bad idea, fire or not."

Staring at the trunks, an idea hits me. I put the damaged trunk in front of the other one and load it up with bodies. I turn it, so the hole's facing the other trunk. Standing at the firepit, the first thing I would see if I came in as an outsider would be the body-trunk. I make sure the other one opens away, toward the beige tent's flaps.

Washing myself off with as little water as I can, I wipe myself on some of the silks and get dressed in the clothes I laid out. I'm sure I heard my feet sigh as I put them in boots that miraculously fit.

I gaze up at the dark-orange-and-red sky. The day's almost done, and I'm beat. That stupid buzzing won't go away either.

Putting the oner's swords and my mana-pistol at one end of the hidden trunk, I climb in and cover myself with the silks. Closing the lid, I make sure that if anyone opens that thing, I'll be able to see them.

I don't remember falling asleep, but my eyes snap open as something slams the trunk. Looks like I've got company.

With the meager morning light that's finding its way into the trunk, I confirm my pistol and swords are just a few inches away.

The sound of a single pair of boots grinding rocks and dirt a few feet away consumes me.

"Open'er up," says a woman. She makes a creepy, giddy noise right after. I know the type, a real jackal.

There's some shuffling about and then a scream. "It's full of freaking bodies!" yells a guy.

There's a thump, probably the lid being slammed shut.

The Jackal laughs. "You're such a durk."

"Yigging piece of—" I hear something crash and the splintering of wood. It's so close to my head, I expect to see a foot come crashing through.

"Stop kicking it you yigging durk. You're getting bits all the way over here," scolds the Jackal.

I take hold of my pistol and concentrate. From my best guess, magic should be working but I don't know if I've got anything in the tank if it comes to that.

"Maybe these kinpaks got robbed after they killed off the spiders?" says the guy as he paces about in front of my trunk.

"Yeah, some guy just came along and thought he'd straighten up, you know, for resale value. Durk," replies the woman.

Everything goes silent for a moment.

"You heard him. Open it," says the Jackal.

I didn't hear anything. Hmm.

"You do it."

"Hey, there's a pecking order, and you're on the bottom. So you open the chest, and I get second pickings."

"That's not fair."

Jackal laughs. "Hey, is that a complaint? Why don't you come over here and complain to the big guy, see what he thinks of that? I remember the last two guys who complained. I don't see them around anymore. But hey, go ahead."

A jackal's never without a leader. But if they're out here, there's got to be at least one enforcer type with them to balance out their pack.

"Fine." The guy raps his hands on the top of my trunk.

My heart's racing, my hands are getting slick. I gently take hold of my mana-pistol.

Don't open it, guy. Just walk away, stand up for yourself, do something else.

Forcing my breathing to be steady, I notice that on top of the buzzing in my head is a strange hum. It's got a wobble to it every now and then.

"Open it!" says the woman.

"I'm getting there!" The boots grind the ground right by my head.

My stomach twists and turns. At first, I think the magic's about to fail, but it's all wrong. I'm about to write it off as nerves when I feel pressure building in my chest, and my mouth has a sudden watery, sour taste. What the yig?

I wipe my sweaty forehead, grimacing as whatever's going on in my chest keeps growing. It reminds me of when I ran into the ghouls.

Gah, this is really freaking uncomfortable.

I try to limit my squirming, but there's no way to get comfortable. For a moment, I think it might be gas. What a surprise that would be, but I know— Yig, what is this? I swear my ribs are being pushed outwards bit by bit.

My face twists into a nasty scowl, my eyes fixed on the thin slice of light coming from the trunk lid.

Stay focused, stay in control. There's more of them than you, and you've got no healing, so that means no mistakes.

"What are you doing?" asks the Jackal. "How is this guy so incompetent? Just open it."

"I'm checking for traps. What, you want me to just open it and get my head blown off?" snaps the guy.

It's getting hot in here.

I'm shaking, resisting the pain that just keeps growing.

Don't move, stay focused.

A wave of nausea hits me. I throw up in my mouth but stop myself from making a mess everywhere. I tighten my grip on my mana-pistol.

Everything goes dark as the guy steps in front of the lid, blocking the slice of light I was getting.

Remember, you covered yourself. He should open it up, see some silks, pull a few, and close it. Don't play your cards too quickly. They'll probably celebrate then plan on carrying it off somewhere rather than staying here and potentially running into wind spiders or something worse. Stay focused, and this could work.

The trunk door twitches.

In a flash of blue from my mana-pistol, a huge hole is ripped through the trunk and the guy opening it. The pressure in my chest halves and I feel light-headed.

The remains of the guy fall backward, a smoking hole through him. Yig, I really screwed this up.

I scramble out of the trunk and crouch down out of sight. Quickly, I remove the swords and put them on my back in their scabbards.

With my back to the trunk, I rub my face with a hand. What the yig do I do now?

I fight the panic and try to breathe. My chest and stomach are still making fun at my expense. What the yig was that? I was just trying to ready myself.

Closing my eyes, I push everything aside and listen. There's no shock or screaming. There's just silence. That's not good. Either they've taken off, which I doubt, or they're trying to figure out their next move because the expendable guy just bit it.

I need a minute to recover, so how do I buy myself time? Well, there's one way.

The back of my mind tries to stop me, but it hasn't got a chance.

After tucking my mana-pistol into the back of my pants, I wave a hand above the trunk. "Hey! I didn't do that to your guy. He does look pretty dead though. I was trapped in that trunk. There was a magical lock on the inside. He couldn't hear me warning him."

Yig, I hope they buy it. I've never been a good liar when I really needed to be.

Licking my lips, I lean forward hoping to catch them saying something. All I get are the sounds of a few pairs of boots scraping about, and tent fabric flapping in the wind as it picks up.

Staring down at the guy, I see he's got pupils, so they're not oners. How come they're so quiet? It's driving me crazy.

My eyes dart about as I'm thinking. I have a vague memory of a mute guy once talking with his hands. Maybe they're doing that. Doesn't really matter; I can't give them too much time to plan.

"I'm going to stand up. You're going to see two swords on my back; they're… just for show," I say, wincing. Maybe I shouldn't have said that. "I just want to walk out of here. You can have the silks and stuff."

I wait for any kind of reply. Again, all I get is boots shifting about. Why isn't the Jackal yammering on at me? Taunting me? I hate it when things are off.

The sound of a rifle being cocked yanks my attention. So they've got someone over to my right who's eager to be dangerous. Good to know. Jackal woman on the left, rifle guy on the right. Alright, let's see what's really out there.

I start standing when my legs go weak and I fall forward on to the trunk, catching myself with my hands.

Closing my eyes for a second, I feel my chest going nuts. I gasp, trying to breathe. My body starts shaking.

"I'm in control here!" I yell at myself, breaking into a full body sweat. I strike myself twice in the chest with my fist; it feels like it helps as I catch a breath.

As whispers of a demonic child's voice enter my head, I realize that I've gone and screwed myself even more. The nice, peaceful guy just yelled about control. Nice, you yigging idiot. But on the other side, I know that someone here is able to use magic.

My chest pain's blocking out any instincts; I feel naked. Straightening up, I carefully reach around behind me and tap my mana-pistol for luck.

Time to go big or go home, and I ain't got a home.

I look up.

There's a guy with a rifle on my right. He's thin and wiry, with a glazed look about him. His shoulder-length black hair's greasy and pasted to his head, and his head is tilted at an odd angle. While he's dressed in a patchwork of leather for a shirt and pants, his rifle looks like serious business; it's a brute.

I put my empty hands out to my sides, palms facing forward, fingers spread apart.

"Let me just get the yig out of here." I slowly move my hands to shield my eyes from the sun.

Over to the left, there are six slaves all chained and huddled together. Even from here, I can tell they're seriously sunburnt.

I make eye contact with one of them, but it's like he doesn't even see me. His gaze just slides right off me.

Studying their faces for a second, I'm disturbed by how placid they seem. There's no fidgeting or crying, no fear, not even misplaced hope that I'm going to free them.

Next up is Jackal, and she's exactly as I imagined her.

Her hair's like a spiky desert bush; her eyes are very sharp and focused. She's got blue paint across her eyes and on the edge of her chin, and she's dressed in a tight jacket and patchwork pants. Hunched over, she's keeping her hands close to her body, but I can see she's deliberately moving her fingers about, maintaining something magical. Her lips are moving in time with the demonic voice in my head.

I follow her gaze and it takes me a second before my brain registers that there's someone there. Yig, how can I miss a seven-and-a-half-foot tall hulk of a man with a blue blindfold and small, white topknot?

After I blink a few times, he finally stands out from the background. They've definitely got something magical going on, and that means the odds are steeply in their favor. For now.

The Blindfold Man is wearing nothing other than a cloth around his waist and rags on his wrists and ankles. He's covered in blue paint and scars. The longer I look at him, the louder the hum in my head gets.

There doesn't seem to be anyone else, just Blindfold Man, Jackal, and the Rifleman. Those odds don't actually seem all that bad, and then I focus on the slaves again.

Who said they're slaves just because they're chained together? They could be anything, even a mythical giant. They could all be armed and ready to take me out.

Bowing my head a little, I shake my head. Why haven't they shot me? If one of my crew was killed, I'd have... actually, I'd have done much the same thing. I'd want to know what I was up against and how much trouble he'd cause.

"I'm going to walk away right now, okay?" I flash my hands out to the side again and lick my lips, shifting my eyes from one of them to the other.

Letting out my breath slowly, I back up two steps and glance over my shoulder at the tent flaps and to make sure I don't slip in the mess of what's left of that guy.

I'm just about to turn and bolt when I catch a twitch on Jackal's face, the sun glinting off the rising rifle, and the Blindfold Man's fists clenching.

A smile breaks across my face as I pull my mana-pistol out and spring off the trunk towards them.

Before I can get a shot off, the Blindfold Man punches the air in my direction and sends me flying backward right through the tent.

Landing hard and upside down, I feel something crack in my chest and a new type of pain introduces itself. "Welcome to the family," I grunt.

Scrambling back to my feet and dashing to the side, a bullet grazes my arm, and then I feel another pass my leg.

For a split second, I think about using the opportunity to bolt, but drop it. I'm certain the Rifleman will pick me off quick and easy, and if he doesn't, then the Jackal's sure to have a surprise up her sleeve. I'm only walking out of this one way, and that's through them.

Bullets fly as I bolt around the outside of the tent, coming up to the blue one where I drop to the ground.

The bullets keep flying. Clearly, someone's expecting me to head for the opening into the campsite. Instead, I go through the flaps and enter the blue tent on all fours, my mana-pistol out in front.

Jackal and Rifleman are scanning about for me. He's got his rifle up at his shoulder, his head still strangely cocked to the side. She's got a weird-looking blade that she keeps passing from hand to hand.

Glancing over at the slaves, two have gone pale and passed out, the others are sitting happily like they're having a freaking picnic. I'm willing to bet that their minds are being screwed with. I almost feel sorry for the poor mana-cattle.

The Blindfold Man's standing in the fire pit, his hands outstretched. What the yig are you doing, searching for me without eyes? Yig, he's starting to point in my direction.

I line up a shot at the Rifleman, but I'm too far away to be sure I can hit him. And if I get him, Jackal and Blindfold Man are going to be on top of me pretty quickly. And that's still assuming that the slaves are just cattle.

An idea hits me, accompanied with a pang of conscience. I shift my aim and take a breath. I can't run the risk of being hit with a fireball or something crazy. Sorry, this isn't personal.

I kill two of the slaves before everyone reacts. The slaves recoil, the Rifleman takes aim, and the Jackal pounces.

Moving over to have the Jackal between the Rifleman and me, I get ready. As she zigs, I squeeze everything I've got through me and manage to clip him in the shoulder.

The Blindfold Man starts lumbering towards me.

One problem at a time.

Jackal leaps into the air, spinning. By the time I catch the glint of her blade, it's going into my chest.

Falling backwards, I'm thrown off by the look of surprise on her face.

"Weslek?" she mutters as she raises a hand to brush off shards of her broken blade.

Hitting the ground with a thud, I glance down at

my bloody chest and see my hands are empty. Yig, I let go of my pistol.

Giving in to something inside, I pull one of the serrated swords off my back and embed it in the side of the Jackal.

Rather than scream, she groans and glares at me with the fury of ten suns. Her lips start moving, and the demonic child's whisper I heard before becomes a shrill yell.

Rolling over and scooping up my pistol in my other hand, I fire. A thin stream of blue fire comes out, but it bounces off a protection in front of her and sets fire to the tent.

Yig, I didn't know someone could do that.

I go to slash at her again with the sword when two meaty hands grab me by the shoulders.

With a roar, the Blindfold Man throws me behind him, end over end.

Whose idea was it to have me take on three guys on my own?

Landing like a discarded rag doll, several ribs crack hard. I lay face down in the dirt, coughing. My body's trembling with fiery torment and searing agony. "Is that all you've got? I can take it," I say through gritted, bloody teeth.

I position my hands to push me up but nothing happens. "Come on." Maybe playing dead is a good idea, at least for a minute.

My breathing's shallow and accompanied by sharp pain.

"At least let's turn around; we're facing the wrong way," I plead with myself. "Where's the fun in dying if you can't see it coming?" My body ignores me and my sarcasm.

Laying there for a minute, I think of the Jackal. Why did her blade shatter? And why am I still breathing? She was aiming for my heart. I should be dead, or at least, dead-ish.

Grunting and grimacing, I reach a hand over to the stab wound and push two fingers in. They don't get far before they run into something sharp and then something hard. I delicately pull out the sharp thing.

It's a shard from the blade, but what then is that hard thing that stopped it?

Shaking my head, I remind myself this isn't over.

Shuffling about like a dying fish, I find the Blindfold Man about fifty yards away with a chain in his hands. He's leading the remaining slaves away, a few rolls of silks in their arms.

After a moment of me staring at him, he stops and faces me. The blindfold over his eyes makes me feel like I'm being glared at by a cyclops.

"I guess… we'll call this one a draw, then?" I say, coughing. "I'm good with that." I'm just thankful that my chest doesn't want to explode anymore.

He points in a direction and then tugs on the chain.

What? Are you warning me? What are you doing?

They just walk.

I consider raising a finger in protest of him taking the silks, but there's no reason to ask Death to reconsider welcoming me just yet.

Licking my lips, I attempt to get up on my hands and knees, but I can't. Every part of my body has had enough. If Jackal or Rifleman are still there, I'm screwed.

episode eight

I lay in the desolate dirt, drifting in and out of consciousness, until my skin feels like it's going to burn off.

Gritting my teeth, I push myself back up onto my knees. I cough and wince, as my broken ribs remind me that they're there. Spitting blood, I shake my head. I really need to get my short-sword back.

Bowing my head and letting my eyes close for a moment, I put a hand over my heart again. There's a preliminary scab. The hard thing in there, did I imagine that?

I trick a leg into coming forward to squatting, and then I push off it to stand. Life wasn't always like this, was it?

Looking about, I can't see the Blindfold Man or his slaves. A strong burnt smell beckons me, and I turn to see that the blue tent is gone.

With an arm wrapped around my side, I stagger to the campsite. I notice the sun's moved a fair amount, showing that I was lying there for a good few hours.

The contents from the trunk I'd been in and that the Blindfold Man didn't take, are all over the place.

I run my tongue along the outside of my teeth as I focus on what's missing. Checking the area, I can't find any sign of the Jackal or Rifleman's bodies, though the two slaves that I killed are there.

"Where did they go?" I scratch my forehead, baffled.

I do another sweep of the area, concentrating on where the Jackal had been, and scoop up my mana-pistol.

Bending down carefully, groaning the whole time, I pick up the hilt of her blade. There doesn't seem to be anything special about it. Studying the area, there are shards of metal around, most of them covered in blood.

So the stabbing was real, but where did she go? The only evidence that she existed is a pool of sticky blood.

"Ah, can't forget that." I pick up the serrated sword and put it back in the scabbard.

I gently stand straight and gaze out at the horizon. I need a plan. No way I can stay here another night. My luck was bad enough the first night. I've got no food, but at least I have some water.

"Water!"

I check through the discarded stuff and find the

water bladder off to one side with a single roll of silks.

Huh. He should have taken both of those, unless he's poisoned the water and trapped the silks.

I open the water and give it a sniff. I can't tell if he did anything to it, but it feels a good deal lighter. Maybe he just took a drink?

Pushing the silk roll with my foot a bit, I don't see anything wrong with it, either.

I laugh and immediately wince from the fiery retribution. "Are you for real, Blindfold Man? Are you trying to tell me we got off on the wrong foot?"

Gazing off in the direction he went, I wonder. Maybe the world's not made of people trying to stab you every second they get, maybe there are some decent people left. And maybe I'm going soft.

I gingerly sling the leather bladder over my shoulder. With gritted teeth, I then dare to pick up the silk roll.

"Gah!" I howl, tears in my eyes. "Mother of Mercy this is yigging wonderful fun."

This is going to be challenging. I've got to find those scavengers and kill them twice for taking my healing sword.

Taking two steps, my body stops. My hands and legs are shaking.

"We're going. There's no option. One step, then another. Now move!"

With an angry grimace of defiance on my face, I head out.

⁂

A few hours later, I drop the empty water bladder. The road seems to continue to go left, go right, rise and fall, and then repeat. The smoke in the distance looks no closer.

Arriving at the top of yet another one of the rolling hills, I'm surprised by what lays before me. It looks like a deep, dry lake bed with a tent city in the middle.

My stomach gurgles as the delightful scent of cooking and spices reaches my nose. A smile cracks my already bloody lips. What I wouldn't give for a real meal.

As I descend into the unexpected oasis, I take in the colors and shapes of the hundreds of tents. They seem well set up, with a three-storey building at their center. What's that looming over the building? I stop in disbelief.

I laugh, not caring about the stinging retribution from my ribs. "I've got to be dreaming, because those look like real, green, leafy trees. I can't remember the last time I saw any, let alone that big."

I spot a caravan of carts descending into the tent city from the opposite side, about a mile away. There's only one road for this place. It doesn't look like much traffic dares come down the steep northern and southern sides.

As I get to the bottom of the lake bed, I'm met with the sounds of people: talking, banging, and whatnot. It makes my skin crawl. This is the first piece of civilization I've come across, and part of me wants to head back into the tranquility of the wasteland.

Upon closer inspection, the tents are pitched haphazardly, some even a foot or two onto the road. The road itself comes to an end at a long row of logs. The logs have iron rods sticking out of them with loops and horses tied to them.

I'm curious if anyone has a levi, and if so, would they dare bring it to a place like this? I'm willing to bet that it'd get ripped off pretty quickly. I'd be tempted, myself.

People are coming and going from the tents; no one's paying me any attention, which I appreciate.

Taking a moment to just watch the bustle around me, it's not too bad. My stomach's relaxing, my heart's calming down, and while my ribs hurt, I'm managing. Even the buzzing in my head's tolerable.

I finally make it up to the horses. Most of them look reasonably healthy, though I quickly spot a few deformities, including one with six legs.

A guy arrives with some hay; another, with water. They fill two of the troughs. There's a number of them down the line, although there's only a dozen horses or so.

I give one of the caretakers a wave, and he hesitates. Eventually, he offers a small wave and flashes a forced smile and gets back to work.

What's that about?

Rolling my shoulders back, and grunting for the millionth time from the rib pain, I keep heading towards the big building. The path winds back and forth, forking every fifty feet, or so it seems.

After a few minutes, I stop, certain I'm lost. The tents are too high for me to see the building or trees.

I massage my temples as a headache asserts itself over top of everything else. There's too much to see, too much to hear, and too much to sell. It's like noise of every kind, and my brain's getting overwhelmed.

"I'll trade for that," says a woman with a heavy accent stepping out of a tent. Her face and hands are weathered and tanned. Her sun-bleached hair's braided and runs past her shoulders. She's wearing a blue-and-white dress, a hilt of something peeking out from behind her back.

I straighten up, squinting at her. "What?"

She points at my legs.

Frowning, I look down and realize I've rested the roll of silk against my legs.

Pointing at the building, I ask her, "Is that place a bar?"

She waves off my question. "I'll trade."

"Okay, fine," I say with a sigh. "What're you offering?"

She studies me for a second, certainly sizing me up. My new clothes may be dirty and a bit roughed up, but at least I don't look like a third-rate beggar as I did before.

"I'll give you... thirty gild," she says. The hesitancy in her face tells me that she's lowballing me.

Hmm. She's likely curious if I'll take it, which would tell her that I found the clothes and have no idea what I'm doing. That could be trouble for me later.

The wrinkles around her eyes tell me that if I counter offer too high, she'll think I'm salvager with no idea of the silk's worth.

The sad truth is I'm the worst of both worlds, as far as I can remember. I don't even know what a gild is. Never heard of it.

Scratching my chin, I shake my head. I go to pick up the silk and wince, a curse slipping out.

"You're injured? I'll give you a good deal," she says, wagging a finger at me and popping into her tent.

I stand there, wondering if she's coming back or not. After a minute, I check that my pistol and swords are still there; they are.

She returns and hands me a blue velvet bag that jingles. "Forty-five and—"

"You," interrupts a menacing voice.

A sideways glance is all I need to recognize the Blindfold Man standing several yards away.

episode nine

Taking the risk of being attacked from behind, I turn my attention away from the big guy and focus explicitly on the trader. "Healing?"

The nervous look in her eye tells me that Blindfold Man's coming over.

"Lady," I snap my fingers in her face.

"Oh, yes." She gives me a pendant.

"This looks like Randmon," I say, staring at it. It's about an inch and a half long and has a bright, shiny, silver-and-gold body. Huh, it looks remarkably like a mouse. Oddly, it's warm to the touch. After pinning it to my vest, I look up but she's gone.

Taking a step backwards, I bang right into the human wall that is the Blindfold Man.

"She pay you a good price?" he asks, his voice deep enough to rattle the bones of the dead.

I chew on my upper lip, noticing the weird wobbling hum is back. Turning around, I give him a good look.

He's a monster of a man, seven-foot-something and pure muscle. He's a quilt of scars, branding and paint. The skin that's not already covered is a dark red-brown. His arms and legs are massive. It's no surprise that he was able to just pick me up and throw me.

There's a satchel sitting mostly behind him, a strap securing it around his waist. Yigging thing would probably be a backpack for me.

Glancing past him, I'm surprised not to see Jackal or Rifleman. There's more to that story. I'm sure of it.

Rubbing the side of my mouth, I look him in the eyes. "To be honest, I can't tell."

He gestures to the velvet bag and I shrug. Opening it, he runs a finger through its contents. "Hmm, you're lucky. There's a lot of scammers around."

He lumbers forward a few yards before turning back to see I haven't moved an inch. Frowning at me, he says, "You coming or not? They've got beer." He points, but I can't see anything; he probably means the building.

"We suddenly friends?" I ask, blinking slowly in case he goes for something.

"I'm just offering a beer." His face is tight and stern.

Out of the corner of my eye, I see a few faces in

tents watching us. I get the impression they're not happy with what's going on, though I'm not sure why.

As I straighten up and raise my chin, trying to give a tough impression, I flinch in pain. I'm sure these tent-types thrive on the weak, and I just showed the wrong cards. I'm better following the Blindfold Man and seeing what he's really got to offer. How much worse could it be?

"Gilds are coins?" I ask.

He nods.

"This a good amount?" I ask, jingling the purse I was given.

He shrugs. "Good enough."

"Then I'll buy the beer."

———

As I follow the Blindfold Man along the winding dirt path between tents, I note how everyone seems to give him no more than a casual glance. Either they're used to seeing him, or it's something else. I'm thinking it's the latter, but I can't think what that might be.

Me, on the other hand, they're giving sideways glares. The hair on the back of my neck's standing up. Twice I reach around to where I've got my pistol tucked into my pants and give it a touch, just to make sure it's there.

There doesn't seem to be any identifiable guards or soldiers, which makes me wonder about two things: first, how they dispense justice, and second, if this place is here year-round or just for a few days.

My head bobs, and I almost tip over. I hadn't realized how exhausted I am. Pain has a way of quietly grinding you down.

I've fallen behind the Blindfold Man; he's almost out of sight. Several people on the path slow down and stare at me. I glare back. Wincing and grunting, I pick up the pace.

We turn a corner in the endless sea of tents and arrive at the three-storey building. Its base is carved stone, probably from something that was already here. The rest is a rich, dark wood.

The place has a lot of windows, which is pretty daring for a tavern. It's filled with loud patrons. There's a steady stream of them coming and going.

Next to the building is a garden unlike anything I can remember seeing before. There's a winding creek with waterfalls that comes down to a pond with colorful fish swimming about. Surrounding all of it is a radiating rainbow of beautiful flowers, and at the back is a cluster of towering trees giving shade to the third-floor patio.

The Blindfold Man taps me on the shoulder with the back of his hand and motions at the tavern's entrance with his head.

"Sorry, I haven't seen anything like that in a while."

I take a step in, and a chill runs down my spine. My eyes dart from face to face, weapon to weapon. I turn back and look at the ridge of the lake bed, but there's nothing. Something's gotten under my skin. Maybe I'm just being paranoid, but then again, the paranoid survive.

"Are you going in or not?" says an irritated guy leading a small party of bright-robe-wearing merchants behind me. "The doorway's not a destination, it's part of the journey. Go in or get out."

I get out of the way and allow myself another moment. Drawing in a deep breath, I brace myself for the stabbing pain, but it doesn't come. Smiling, I tap the pendant. "Maybe this actually does something. Huh."

The place has standing tables everywhere and stairs in the far left corner heading up. At the far end is a bar with a brass rod to rest a foot.

The Blindfold Man's at the bar. As I approach, he lifts his head and faces me. I feel him acknowledging my presence, and it's creepy.

As I get two-thirds of the way to the bar, I bump into someone leaning against a standing table. Just as the apology is about to escape my lips, I notice the woman opposite him has blond hair with green tips.

Without a thought, I put my arm around the neck of the guy and whip out my mana-pistol, putting it right in the woman's face. "Where's my yigging short sword?"

In the blink of an eye, the woman reaches over, hits my hand with two fingers, and yanks the pistol. Putting it right in front of her, she covers it with her hands and gives a worried glance around.

Impressive.

A scruffy woman from another table leans over. "You know the rules. Best you be stopping all of this or they're going to be dropping you like flies." She gives us a scowl and goes back to her table.

I let her friend go and massage my hand where she hit it, all the while wondering who 'they' are.

Glaring at the woman salvager, I reach for my mana-pistol, but she pulls it closer to her.

I grind my teeth. "Lady, if you want to continue breathing, you're going to return all of my property in the next six seconds."

"We, ah… we can't do that," says her buddy, rubbing his neck.

Her icy blue eyes shift from me to him and back.

"And why's that? Got a death wish?" I ask, my face twitching. "I don't have time for this. I don't care about any yigging rules. I'm done here." I start reaching for a vest pocket that's got nothing.

"Wooo, stop," says the guy.

The woman's glaring at me. One of her hands has disappeared below the table.

Looking at the guy again, I get the routine. He's the distractor; she's the actor. I can't let them play me.

"I've blown up bigger places than this and walked away before." I stare at the woman.

Slowly, I move my hand over, and she releases the pistol to me. I immediately put it away, checking that no one's paying us too much attention. "Where's my short sword?"

"We sold it," says the guy, his wide eyes moving all about like they're loose in his head.

"It was a contract. We delivered," says the woman.

I scan the crowd and scratch the back of my head. "Where do I find the person you sold it to? And how did they know about it? About me?"

"Everyone's heard the story of the stabbed statue —ah, you. I mean... I first heard it years ago."

"Years?" I furrow my brow and lean into the guy. "What the yig are you talking about?"

"Hey," barks the woman, stepping around the table and grabbing me by the vest. "We did a job. Law of the land: We take, we keep." She lets me go and pats my chest. "If you have an issue, take it up with the Wizard of—"

It's like a bomb of silence goes off, radiating from her outwards. In two seconds, the entire place has fallen silent, and everyone is looking at us—no, her.

"We have to go," she says to her friend, taking him by the arm.

I stand in her way, shaking my head. "Who?"

Someone slaps a hand down on my shoulder from behind and comes up close to my ear. The bristles of the stranger's beard scratch the side of my face. "They're leaving without another word. You want to bring a Scourge Patrol down on us? The type of people she's thinking of, they have ears. And the one in particular near here, she's said to show up personally when anyone says her name. So, best they go because chances are a Scourge is already on its way to kill them. And I don't know about you, but I'm not keen on dying today."

"I just need to know who's got my stuff."

The man gives me a shove, and the scavengers make their way around me.

"I think they told you enough," he says as I turn around, getting a good look at him. He's about my size, orange beard, and darker orange hair. "Get a drink; move on. We all have stuff that we lose, it's what we do about it that matters."

I watch in frustration as the scavengers exit the tavern. Flashing my palms and fingers apart at the guy, I watch the place liven up quickly.

Rubbing my temple, I make my way to the bar. The buzzing and hum in my head have teamed up and are chewing on the edge of my sanity. I need to find some medicine or something.

The Blindfold Man's standing there with some suspicious elbow room on either side of him. It makes me wonder if there's been problems before and if that's why no one pays any attention to the guy who sticks out like a rock among eggs. He lifts his head a touch as I arrive and slides over.

Resting my elbows on the counter, I put a foot up on the brass rail.

The green glass he's got in his meaty hands looks like it's meant for a child.

"I don't mean to be too rude, but why are we here?" I ask him, staring at the shelves of colorful bottles across from me.

He tilts his head back and finishes off his drink. "You were the statue in the white sand?"

Peering over my shoulder to see if anyone's listening, and satisfied that there isn't, I nod. "Apparently. How long was I out there?"

"I heard the story about three years ago. No more

than ten, I think. Don't know; you could have been covered in sand. Mind you, the floating city fell around here seven years ago. Did that have anything to do with it?"

Something about what he's saying feels off. I don't know if he's lying, stretching the truth, or leaving things out.

I wipe the edges of my mouth and catch the eye of the bartender, getting a nod as his promise to return shortly.

Shrugging, I stare at the colorful bottles on the shelves opposite me. "I don't know. Don't remember much." I get a sense he's studying my reaction somehow.

"We're similar, you and I," he says. "I wasn't always like this."

Narrowing my eyes at him, I wonder what he means and what he knows about me. I'm positive we've never met before. "Where are your friends by the way?" I ask. "The crazy lady and the guy with the rifle. I didn't see their bodies."

"Friends? They're no friends of mine," he scoffs. "But they have to listen to me. They live in here." He taps the side of his head. "For now."

The bartender puts drinks in front of us and moves on. I frown at the glass and then at him as he scuttles away. "I didn't even get to order."

"You don't order here," says the Blindfold Man. "He decides and you pay." Downing his drink in one shot, the Blindfold Man motions for me to pay.

Taking out a few coins, I put them down. He rolls his finger until I've put enough, which is about half what I was paid.

"Guess I didn't get that good of a deal." I put the coins away.

Giving the Blindfold Man a once over, I can't figure out what his game is. "You're not making a lot of sense."

He taps his chest. "The broken blade, killing one of my inner demons with a mana shot from your pistol." He taps his chest again, this time I notice a scar. I rub my own without thinking.

"You're a—" I stop, the hair on the back of my neck's standing straight up.

I back up a step, and he straightens up. Turning to look at the front door, I watch as a hush spreads over the room. It looks like I'm not the only one picking up on something.

A merchant woman runs into the tavern and one word lights the place up in a panic: "Scourge!"

Someone elbows me in the chest by accident, and I stumble backward against the bar.

My head's spinning, and the buzzing forces me to close my eyes and brace myself. Everything's slipping away.

"We don't have much time," says a gruff, accented woman's voice behind me. She pats me on the shoulder.

My eyes are closed, and I'm rubbing my temples. I've got that weird feeling again. My head's a mess, which is nothing new, but the little bits of memory that I'm picking up feel like someone else's.

Opening my eyes, I gaze out at smoke rising from the far side of a city. The wind's bringing the smell of burnt flesh wrapped in devastation. Flames are raging, though the fire looks surgically contained.

I wrench a memory loose. I've seen this before. "They hit the western district?" I ask over my shoulder.

"Yeah," replies a man. "Supposedly they sealed it with wards yesterday morning then sent oners in after. In the evening, they sent in three Scourge Patrols and laid waste to everyone. No exceptions."

"Oners don't work that way," I say shaking my head. "They're lying."

"And how would you know?" says an older man. He sounds irritated and anxious.

Glancing down, I see that I'm wearing a dusty, black, long coat. My fingers are gloved, and I've got a hood up.

Lifting my head and turning around, I see that the three people behind me are dressed the same way. It's odd. I can see them, but I can't feel their presence; I feel alone. I'm tempted to take my gloves off to see if there's a mana-residue on the coat, but I already know the answer.

The guy on the left of the trio is muscular and shorter than the guy in the middle, whose got some white beard showing. The woman's on the right side, her long, dark hair showing.

In the distance, there's a steady stream of shiny objects rising up to, and coming down from, the floating city far above.

I can hear levi-car traffic off in the distance, but the immediate area sounds eerily quiet.

We're on the roof of the tallest building around, and it looks just as bad as I'm sure the undercity's western district will look tomorrow. Maybe the Wizard had this place hit recently. I don't know.

"Quickly, let's get this over and done with," says the woman. She's anxious. I can hear it in her voice, but her hand gestures are even more telling. She moves to stand apart from the other two, so that we form a strange triangle.

"There's been word that our…" The muscular man hesitates.

"You're safe to say anything," says the bearded, older man. "These garments protect us from all eyes and ears for a few hours yet."

The muscular man paces back and forth. "If I get caught for saying anything, I'm going to kill you."

The bearded man shrugs. "We'll all be dead if that happens. The Wizard of Banareal is a deeply paranoid and vindictive man."

There's an uncomfortable silence as everyone waits a few seconds to see if anything happens.

"Alright." The muscular man stops moving. "There's word that the High Acolyte may have been arrested. I have a friend who spoke to someone."

"That's not fact," says the bearded man.

"No, but it fits with what I heard. The question is if it's because our ruler suspects him of being a part of the growing rebellion, or if it's treachery at the hands of the next in line for his position," says the woman.

"Great," I mutter, rolling my shoulders and glancing about at the undercity skyline. I've got a growing feeling that I should run, like an itch you can't scratch that keeps getting worse and worse.

"What about you?" I say to the bearded man. "Got

anything?"

He turns to the muscular man and then to the woman before answering. "I learned that, a few weeks ago, they cleared out the bottom floors of the palace. There's speculation that it's to expand the magical weapons program, but I have no proof or confirmation. It could be nothing." His head lowers, a sense of fear and burden radiating from him.

"That's not fact either," snaps the muscular man.

"No, I suppose not."

"This is about piecing together bits of a puzzle: Some will fit, some won't. We stay focused on pulling this all together, and we'll be better for it. We can't do this alone." I'm surprised that blurted out of me, and I wonder what I was doing before showing up on the roof top.

I stare at the orb's silver streak. Why does this look familiar?

"What about you?" asks the woman, pointing at the orb. "That thing tell you anything?"

Putting it away, I shake my head, figuring it's better that they don't know. Frowning, I try to remember if I've already unlocked its secrets or not—and if not, I'm really screwed.

"We've got support; we're not alone," I say, wondering what else I can tell them.

"From whom?" presses the woman, taking a step

toward me.

Taking another breath, something comes to me. "A librarian said that the High Acolyte would be arrested."

"You've been in contact with a librarian? You've killed us all. Which wizard did it have allegiance to?" asks the bearded man, trembling.

"It was the free librarian," I say, my hand out to calm them. "The High Acolyte is key, and we need to have him rescued."

"If the Wizard has arrested him, there's no hope of that," says the muscular man. "It's done."

"I agree," says the woman. "If our ruler's hidden him away, then the old man's as good as dead."

"I know where he is," I say, biting my lip. I probably shouldn't have said that. The hair on the back of my neck and arms suddenly stands up, and I pull back from the group.

"What are you doing?" asks the woman.

"I don't know... I just..." Raising my chin, I put my hands back in my pockets. "We need to get the old man out of the Wizard's lab, and the only way we're going to do that's with him not being alive. That way, we can slip him past all the protective wards."

"You want to kill him?" says the muscular man, shaking his head, one hand out and one right in my face. "You're insane. And what, just bring him back to life?"

"Basically, yes."

He scoffs and shakes his head angrily. "You're crazy."

My head jerks back and forth as I fight against the urge to keep talking.

"Are you well?" asks the bearded man.

"There's a plan. I don't have all of it, but I know it involves getting a smith who is really proficient with enchantments." As the words leave my lips, my head starts to hurt. I put pressure against one of my temples.

"What kind of enchantment?" asks the woman.

I shrug as my body and my will wrestle. My stomach's working up a storm. I thrust a hand in my pocket and grab on to the orb. My heart's racing.

The sound of a levi-car crashing nearby pulls all of our attention.

"It's in the middle of the road; what did it smash into?" The bearded man's leaning over the edge with me. "There's nothing there."

"It's a magical barrier," answers the woman. "They know we're here."

Glancing over my shoulder, I see the muscular guy take off. I want to run after him, but my body forces my gaze up. "The sky. They come from the sky," I recall.

Shiny halos are descending towards us.

"It's a single, large Scourge Patrol."

"How could you know that?" asks the bearded man.

"I remember things," I say, swallowing hard and looking over the edge as some of the halos land, revealing lightning-rifle-carrying soldiers.

The woman reaches out and touches my arm. "The other man betrayed us, didn't he?"

They don't give me time to answer as they take off for the stairs.

Bowing my head, I know it won't do them any good.

I take off my gloves; my hands are sweaty. The orb slides around in my hand as if it's alive. "Think! How does this go down?"

Holding the orb up to my mouth, I hear myself speak words and then feel the thoughts being pulled from my mind.

A lightning weapon crackles down below. I don't need to see it to know that the muscular man just received his reward for treachery.

The orb shimmers, and I sense that it's full. It's weird. I feel like I should be sick or something, but I'm not.

I'm about to throw it when I blank on who the yig I'm going to send it to.

Out of the corner of my eye, I see a form land on the far end of the rooftop. It's wearing a dark-grey robe with glowing yellow detailing.

I know what that is. That's an acolyte and no rookie.

Soldiers start streaming onto the roof from the stairs. The twirling sound of their weapons powering up fills the air.

"This is where I die," I mutter, wiping my mouth, my hand shaking. In a desperate move, I throw the orb. "But not this time."

The five soldiers take up their positions, their lightning rifles all pointing at me. Their weapons crackle with blue, yellow, or red electricity. Part of me braces for the sound of thunder, wishing I had the same protection all of them have stuffed in their ears.

Half of the soldiers have armored plates hovering over various parts of their body, the other half are wearing standard, reinforced vests.

The acolyte steps off the edge of the building, white wisps of air underneath its feet.

Their confident positions and look in each of the soldier's eyes tells me they've been working together for a while. Everyone knows their role; everyone knows how this is supposed to go down.

The sound of weapons firing in the background tells me that at least one of my co-conspirators is giving them a challenge. Sadly, I don't care which one because I know it won't make a difference.

It takes me a few seconds, but I figure out which of the soldiers is the captain. He's second to the end on the right. Perfect.

I watch as the orb arcs in the air, finally turning to head back towards me.

One of the soldiers turns to see what I'm looking at. I can feel the squad's irritation at the newbie's lack of discipline.

The captain barks, and the newbie smartens up. Every soldier has the same dead-eyed expression. Their devotion to hierarchy almost makes them oners; at least, that's what I'm hoping for.

I open my hand, sweat dripping off the edge of my nose. My eyes are focused on the orb as it speeds towards me.

My body's rebelling with everything it's got. My stomach's sending volleys up my throat which I won't let out, my face is twitching nervously, and there's a tremor that runs through me. Sorry, but I'm jumping off the cliffs of insanity.

I spring towards the captain and drop to my knees, one hand open and down low.

Everyone moves and yells at me to freeze.

I put my other hand out, fingers spread apart. Then it happens.

The orb strikes the captain right in the back of the head, emitting a sickening crack as his neck bends unnaturally.

The sense of confusion among the soldiers is

immediately palpable. Everyone turns to look at the one I figure's the next in command.

The instance it snaps into my hand, I throw the orb again and drop to the ground in front of the next in line. I shut my eyes tight and scream with my mind for the orb to return.

My heart is beating like a rabbit's; I can hardly breathe. I don't know why I'm doing this, but I can't get away from the feeling it's important.

The soldier grabs me by my hood and hauls me to my feet. He shoves a pistol into my ribs hard.

Opening my eyes, I stare at his floating armored plates. "Why do they only armor you in the front?"

The soldier's intense stare is replaced with horror as the orb crushes the middle of his spine.

The orb rolls around the edge of his body as it finds its way to my hand. Pushing off of him, I let myself fall backwards as two soldiers fire, one of them hitting their former team mate.

I try to toss the orb again, but this time it just falls to the ground. Grabbing it as I fall to the ground, I see the acolyte land a few feet away and freeze.

"Enough of this," she says, her voice eerie and twisted. The acolyte flicks her wrist. I'm sent spinning in the air, landing hard at the edge of the building.

I can taste blood in my mouth, and I can't see properly.

The soldiers fold in around the acolyte, who floats towards me, my level of panic rising with every inch closer she gets.

One thought keeps going through my head: *She cannot get the orb.* Desperate, I roll off the side of the building.

The world spins violently until I stop, all of a sudden, in mid-air. I'm turned over, and I stare up at the acolyte who gets closer and closer.

"Hey!" I hear below me.

I crane my neck. It's the woman from earlier, my co-conspirator. I toss her the orb.

To my surprise, it makes it to her.

The acolyte lets go of me and runs after the woman on invisible stairs.

Hitting the ground hard, I get the wind knocked out of me. Yig, I don't need this. Pushing myself up on my hands and knees, the world spinning, I grab on to a garbage can and then a doorframe.

I stagger for the first few steps but then I regain my balance. I should take off, but that woman's dead. Like a lunatic, I chase after the acolyte.

Arriving in the nick of time, I find the woman in a dead end alley, the acolyte taking the final step to the ground.

The woman spots me, and I point at the floating city.

She throws the orb.

At first, it starts going up, and then it arcs straight into the hand of the acolyte. She then points at the woman with her other hand, making her burst into flames so fierce they knock me to the ground.

The acolyte pulls me into the air. A tendril from the robe reaches over and pulls my hood back. What new horror is this?

"How could you get involved in this? How could anyone?" yells the acolyte. "Our cause is righteous."

The robe's hood parts, revealing a beautiful, dark-skinned woman with blond hair. She stares deeply into my eyes, and I feel the fury and disappointment.

"The Wizard's building a bomb. It will one day—"

"It doesn't matter. Whatever you have to say, it is his Oneness's prerogative," she says, the edges of her mouth curled up in a snarl.

My body starts to heat up.

"I need to know everything," she says as she places a hand on my forehead. I notice she has the orb in the other.

Pain erupts from everywhere.

I trip and fall, my chin smacking into something before I get a grip. The sharp, physical pain vanquishes the fiery nightmare that had been there a moment ago. My eyes snap open, my tongue picking up the taste of copper from where I just bit it.

I stand up and lean on the bar. The Blindfold Man is standing beside me, giving me a sideways look, a fresh drink in his mammoth, dirty hands.

Bowing my head, I listen to the room, which is in a panic. Frowning, I think hard, and the memories ride in. "Scourge. There's a Scourge Patrol coming, isn't there?"

The Blindfold Man gives me a sideways look and nods. "Everyone's searching for their passports. No passport, they either kill you on the spot or arrest you. They don't do much arresting," he says, taking a calm sip of his drink.

My heart starts pounding. Wiping the sweat off my lips, I turn to see people rifling through belongings, fighting, and some bolting out the door.

The look on their faces tells me the Blindfold Man's not exaggerating, or at least not by much.

"Where's the floating city?" I ask, looking about as I rummage through my memories, finding nothing. "You don't get Scourge Patrols without a floating city."

He lifts his chin a bit, his expression shedding its friendliness. "Where have you been? The fallen city's near here, and their Wizard's planning on rebuilding, reinventing, and rediscovering everything that made the old world so legendary."

Something he said is bothering me, making me want to take off, though I can't put my finger on it. I know better than to question my instincts. "I've got to go."

He whips out a hand and grabs my arm in a steel grip. Without releasing the drink from his other hand, he forces me back to the bar.

"You're not going anywhere," he says calmly, taking another sip of his drink.

"Let go of me." I put an arm up to grab the hilt of a serrated sword.

He yanks me forward, bringing me right up to his face. The hum that surrounds him becomes discordant screeches.

"That wouldn't be a good move." He frees his drink and grabs something under the wrist rags. He drops two shiny stones.

Before they hit the ground, the Jackal and Rifleman appear. They look exactly like they did when I saw them last time, minus the leg and shoulder wounds.

The Jackal rolls her shoulders and cracks her neck. "Just enjoy your drink and your last minutes of freedom, you weslek freak," she says with a smile. "Make a move, and we'll kill ya. And if we don't, then everyone here will. The Wizard lets this place exist. There's no chance anyone's going to let you violate any of the rules, because they all know it could mean they all get killed. The Wizard's done it before."

Why does she keep saying wizard? Am I just paranoid to think that a real wizard could hear or have spies about that would send word back? I notice a few patrons watching, their ears having perked up at the word weslek.

Looking at the Rifleman, he's got that dead-eyed stare. His head is bowed and tilted to the side. I half-expect drool to be running down the side of his face.

I put my free hand on the counter, and the Jackal pats me on the back, flagging the bartender. She hasn't removed my swords or mana-pistol, which makes me wonder just how much confidence they have in themselves and the other patrons. I'm not eager to find out.

A satisfied smile cracks across the Blindfold Man's face as he tilts his head back and finishes off his drink, his vice-grip keeping me in place.

"So, what's the deal?" There's got to be an angle I can play.

Jackal chuckles while the Rifleman just stands there oblivious to the world. "Why? You think you're going to offer a better one? Not going to happen."

For a moment, I wonder if she's real, but then the bartender arrives and puts a drink in front of her.

"Maybe you've got a long-lost friend, and they offered a reward for you," says Jackal, a twisted giggle escaping her. "Or someone who owes you."

The bartender won't look me in the eye. His expression tells me he knows what's going down. I wonder if they're bounty hunters of a sort. Interesting crew, if that's the case.

Looking out the corner of my eye, I see the earlier panic's giving way to relief as people clutch small bundles of prized paper. No one's paying attention to us. They must be used to all kinds of things going down and shrug it off unless it threatens the rules.

In the reflection of her glass, I see the Jackal's got a devilish grin. She's eating up the fear and confusion playing out on my face.

Rubbing my forehead with the tips of my fingers, I shake my head and turn to the Blindfold Man. "You said we were alike."

He shifts his stance to face me. "You can hear it, can't you? My hum."

I stare at him, thinking. After a moment, I nod.

"I didn't know you were like me until her blade broke. You've got no sound, but I know it's there. It's just higher, pure. Like the song of stars."

What's this guy been drinking?

Frowning, I think back to when I put my fingers into my chest and felt a solid thing inside. Is this guy saying that he's a weslek?

"Why would someone want me?"

The Blindfold Man laughs, his expression betraying his bitterness. "You're a real weslek, an original."

"A what?"

Jackal forces a laugh and slaps my back. "He doesn't even know? What a durk."

I fake smile. "Humor me. I'm not going anywhere." My eyes narrow as I pick up demonic whispers in the background. It could be an acolyte with the Scourge, or it could be any one of the merchants—no way to know. It does remind me, however, that I'm running out of time.

Blindfold Man lifts his head, giving me a once over. I'm curious how he sees the world, but there's no chance I'm going to get answers to that.

"She's had a bounty on you for quite a while, they say even before she became Wizard of the Fallen City. She's got people who can hack together anything, but a real weslek? A perfect soul? That she can't do... yet." He taps my chest, right over my heart. "And the prize is right there. That crystal masterpiece is what she wants, and I'm giving it to her."

He turns back to his drink. "Not that I ever met her."

"Who is she?" I ask.

"The Wizard of the Fallen City, you yigging durk," says the Jackal, slapping me in the back of the head. "Can you believe this guy?" She downs her drink.

I bite my tongue and stare at the ground. The last thing I need to do is blow this situation up, but I'm not seeing a lot of options.

Taking a deep breath, I note that my ribs don't hurt anymore. Maybe that mouse pendant is actually doing something.

"What about you?" I ask him. "What's your deal?"

"I'm your freak cousin. The Wizard's going to create all the best from before the Great War. I'm just one of the steps along the way. The best of what she's been able to do, I'll have you know. The only one to go free, too," he says, the edges of his mouth turned up in pride. He taps me in the chest with the back of his hand.

Whispers at the back of my mind are saying the Scourge is coming, but it's not what they're expecting. The hair on the back of my neck's standing straight up.

If I don't get out of here, I'm going to be pulled apart by some crazed wizard and her flunkies. Not really what I had planned for my day. Time to blow things up.

I smile at the Jackal.

She smiles back, arching both eyebrows in suspicion.

I keep smiling, my stare becoming an intense glare. I wait until I see her eyebrows twitch as confusion sets in, then a touch of fear. She leans away from me.

Perfect.

I slap my free hand down on the Blindfold Man's anchoring arm and reach deep down within myself.

I need to find that part of me that drained Ania's dying friend. Come on. I'm going to rip the life out of this yigging kinpak.

My eyes go wide as I feel him start to pull life from me. A menacing grin starts spreading across his face, as if I've just unlocked a part of him.

Pain shoots up my arm and into my spine; his deep, discordant, hum invades my thoughts. As I push myself, I watch as his grin melts into a grimace of anguish.

His hum breaks apart into a soul-shredding assault of sharp sounds, like musical instruments being hit with rocks. I can feel it in my teeth.

Jackal starts pounding on my back. The Rifleman looks up, his eyes filled with anger. His hands are moving about himself, likely from hidden weapon to hidden weapon, unsure what would be allowed in the tavern.

A grin cracks through my pained face. I guess I got their attention.

The Blindfold Man's lips give way to yellow, gritted teeth. "Is that all you've got?"

"We're not done yet." I imagine willing a river to me. Waves of excruciating pain start hitting me, but I don't care. It's an old friend by now.

"I'll rip your heart out!" Blindfold Man tries to move, but his limbs fail him, and he falls to the floor. I stay with him.

Every nerve in my body is on fire, and I'm starting to wonder if I can keep going.

I'm momentarily distracted as Rifleman dissipates into a red mist and flows into Blindfold Man.

"No!" screams the Jackal. I catch her following suit.

I can't feel my heart beating. I can't catch a breath. The edge of my vision's going black.

Suddenly there's a sharp and distinct cracking sound. The fury in the Blindfold Man's eyes slips away, replaced by mortal fear.

"Die weslek," he whispers. He pulls back a fist, which starts glowing red.

The image of the wesleks chained to the bottom of the floating city flashes before me, giving me an idea.

As his fist makes its way towards me, I push all of my life and mana into him. He erupts in screams. He transforms into white sand and falls apart.

I slump, smacking my head on the wooden floor.

A sense of dread washes over my weary body and mind. The Scourge... I've got to get out of here.

Get up.

Don't black out. Get up!

episode fourteen

With a primordial growl, I haul myself to my
hands and knees. My hands, arms, legs... they're all
numb. The periphery of my vision's all black, but
there's no way I'm falling apart now. Something's
coming for me, and I'm going to give it the best fight I
can.

I try to get up, but nothing happens. Okay, I'll wait
a second. A chuckle escapes out of me as I think of
how many times I've found myself in this position.

For a moment, I can picture the Old Man's face
and him telling me how it doesn't matter how many
times you get knocked down, as long as you get up
one more time. It fills me with hope, and then his
image is gone.

I hear someone come over from a nearby table.
The boots are worn but still in great condition,
probably expensive once upon a time. The stink of hot
breath and sweaty feet hits me hard as that someone
crouches down beside me.

"Are you okay? I don't know what happened

between you and… whatever that was, but it seems to have resolved. Do you need help?"

With one eye open, I look at him. His skin's dark and leathery, his beard white like snow, and his face is honest. He's clutching papers in one hand; it must be his passport.

"Been better," I say, coughing. "I've got a bad habit of ending up the floor of bars feeling like crap."

He chuckles and gives me a pat on the back.

A dark thought crosses my mind. I hate to do it, but I've got to get out of here.

As he goes to stand up, I grab him by the collar.

"Help a man up?" I ask, offering a pained smile.

"Sure," he replies hesitantly. He grabs on to me and helps me stand.

I hold on to him and shoot a glance over at the bar's doorway. People are watching anxiously, arms folded, pacing. They must be able to see the Scourge soldiers.

That buzzing from a while ago tears through my thoughts. I shake my head furiously.

If that's my conscience trying to put up a fight, then I'm sorry. I don't know where you came from, but a man's got to survive.

I punch the good Samaritan in the stomach. As he goes down, I elbow him in the neck, take his passport, and stuff it in my pants pocket. For good measure, I give him a soft kick in the ribs and glare at the people who are wondering what's going on. "No one steals from me."

As people start to swarm around him, I storm out the door. I can hear the voices of surprise and confusion changing to compassion and anger. I've got about ten seconds to get clear of this place before they come hunting for me.

Stepping outside, I see a lineup of merchants and the like. There are four Scourge soldiers with a captain, identified by yellow stripes on the arm of his dark-grey uniform. They're checking people's passports and quizzing them one at a time.

A soldier looks up at me as I turn and walk away from them. "Hey, get in line!"

I flash the passport and keep walking.

"Hey!" He starts following me.

"I've got a passport. Right here! I'm late!" I reply. I'm tempted to stop and show him, but I'm afraid if they are looking for me, they'll know what I look like.

Part of me thinks I'm just being paranoid, that they aren't here for me. This is just a bad coincidence. I hate coincidences.

Rounding a corner, I bolt, weaving through the people coming and going.

"He stole my friend's passport!" I hear in the distance.

The trail between the tents curves back and forth endlessly. The only thing I know is that the angry voices are still behind me, and that's all that matters for now.

I slide to a stop as I come to a dead end. For some reason, my attention's drawn upwards. Far above, in the middle of the deep blue sky, are a few birds, circling. It seems innocent enough, but my gut's telling me otherwise.

Rather than double back, I draw one of the serrated blades and enter a tent. It's empty. I quickly sift through the belongings, but nothing useful jumps out at me.

I slash through the back of the tent and then into the next one. Thankfully, it's empty as well. Again, there's nothing useful lying about. Stepping out of the tent, I'm back on a trail. I put the blade away and start hustling.

Coming to a fork, there's a group of merchants to the north, arguing. I head south.

The tension in the air is getting feverish. The glances of bewilderment from passersby are becoming stares of concern. If I don't find my way out soon, they're going to be roused to action. The last thing I need to do is to try and fight my way out of this place.

A few minutes later, I find myself in another dead end. "Yig! How do you get out of this place?"

I'm a sweaty mess. Putting my hands on my hips, I look up, trying to catch my breath.

There are about ten birds overhead. My gut's not liking it, not liking it at all. I'd swear that I have to squint when looking at them.

The buzzing in my head spikes sharply. My hands start twitching. "Enough bird watching. Get out of here you idiot."

As I run through an intersection, I catch a glimpse of dark grey out the corner of my eye. It's immediately followed by the sound of heavy footfalls and lightning rifles powering up. I don't know how I know the sound, but it doesn't matter. I need to stay focused. All I need to do is outsmart the soldiers and outrun my bad luck. Shouldn't be a problem… yeah, right.

Arriving at another crossroads, a dozen people turn to look at me. I duck into a tent only to find this one's occupied.

A long-haired woman pulls a revolver off a table and points it right at my head.

"Get out," she says, fury in her eyes.

"I'm just—"

"Save it! I know everyone who comes through here, and you," she says stabbing the air with her revolver, "I ain't ever seen before."

I put my hands out to the side a bit. My cheeks are

red and dripping with sweat. "Please, just give me a second to think, then I'm out of here."

She pulls the hammer back. "You aren't going to do much thinking with your brains out of your head. Now get out!"

"I don't have a passport, and the Scourge's chasing me," I say, bowing my head and looking up at her.

"I'm willing to bet that you're the reason they're here."

My heart's pounding so hard I can barely hear.

She renews her grip on the revolver. "Get out! If the Scourge catch me harboring someone without a passport, then they're going to drag me off too."

Lowering my gaze, I shake my head. I can't see a way out of this. Slowly, I turn around and take a step.

"Swords and... what kind of pistol is that? Mother of Mercy! HELP! I've got some frea—"

I spin around grab her, putting my hand over her mouth.

Her weapon goes off, and I immediately start hearing whispers of demonic children as well as shouts from outside. This is going to get very bad, very fast.

Yig, yig, yig. Now what? There's no way that I'm killing her, because if I start down that road, this place is going to become a heap of bodies with mine lost somewhere in the mix.

I shove the woman backwards and take out my mana-pistol, pointing it at her head. She tosses her revolver on the floor.

I motion with my other hand for calm. "I just need a second to think, and then I'm out of here."

episode fifteen

Lowering my pistol to point at her feet, I back away. As the flaps of the tent touch my back and legs, I notice a pile of dirty laundry beside me. A torn-up brown shirt is on top.

"May I take that?" I ask.

"You're asking me about a rag? At gun point?" She angrily waves me off.

I give her a quick smile. "Thanks." Wrapping my mana-pistol in the shirt, I step out of the tent.

The trail's filled with people all either scared or angry. A group's going from tent to tent, trying to figure out where the gunshot came from.

Hurrying away, I end up in at another yigging fork. I'm so tempted to take out a sword and just start cutting tents in a straight line.

I nearly jump out of my skin as thunder booms several times. Wait, that's not thunder. Those are lightning rifles. The Scourge has started killing people.

Wiping my face with both hands, I pace back and forth. "Everything looks the yigging same." I rub my temples. "Yigging buzzing."

Pressure's starting to build in my chest, though I'm wondering if I'm on my way to having a heart attack.

"Everything just stop! I need to think!"

Making sure no one's watching, I slip my mana-pistol out of the shredded shirt and into the back of my pants. I pull my shirt and vest over it. Then, I wrap the shredded shirt around my head. Bending down, I get some dirt and rub it on my cheeks and the rims of my eyes.

It's not much of a disguise, but if people aren't paying attention, maybe I've got a chance.

A man comes up the path and stares at me, terrified.

"Are they coming?" I ask.

He doesn't move or say a thing.

"Are there Scourge soldiers around?"

He tilts his head up, his expression getting only more intense.

I snap my fingers at him. Nothing.

Whatever, I don't have time for this.

A minute later, I come across a young, bald woman, a middle-aged man, and an old woman with curly white hair. Crumpled papers lay at their feet, likely their passports.

They're all staring straight up. Their expressions are variations of the man I just disregarded.

Touching my forehead and cheeks, I feel hot, flush. There's a sick air of familiarity. I don't want to gaze up, but I can't help myself. Shielding my eyes from the blistering sun, I gaze up. There's a large flock of birds, moving in a giant circle.

"What are they?" I ask, sniffing. It smells like burnt barbecue.

The old woman takes a gulp of air, but her voice is shaky. "It's the end."

"What are you talking about?"

She glances at me, and then back up at the sky. Her eyes are filled with tears, her lip quivering. "I should have left with my son this morning."

I study the other two. There's a sense of doom in their eyes.

At the back of my mind, I swear there's a memory locked in a cage, screaming to get out. For me to get out.

I'm about to ask them what's going on, what are those birds, when a demonic voice enters my mind.

I shut my eyes tightly and stumble back and forth, my hands on my temples pushing tightly. Unlike the child-like voices I've heard before, this one is strong, commanding, and a woman's. It takes me a moment before I'm steady.

"Passports, now," commands a soldier standing only three yards away.

Yig, I didn't see him coming.

He's got a young, bearded face, and a brawny build. Both hands are firmly on his five-foot long lightning rifle. Its outer shell is black metal with a wooden interior. There are two silver-blue bars of crushed charging crystals that run from the barrels to near the trigger, where there's a rectangular charging crystal.

"Hey," I say to the guard pointing at the sky. "What are those? Why's everyone freaking out?" My voice is shaky. I gaze up and feel my soul become infected with dread. I swear there's fire trailing the birds as they move.

I watch as the soldier glances upward and loses all composure. "Holy freak. The Captain said they wouldn't start until we were out of here."

He lets the rifle go slack and pulls out two rectangular stones. One he holds up to his mouth. "Captain! Captain!" He's sweating bullets.

I grit my teeth as the demonic woman's voice gets louder, and the buzzing becomes a roar. My sanity's being eaten away.

Screw this, I can't take it. I take one of the swords off my back and throw it at the soldier. As it sails through the air, I rush him.

The soldier drops the stones and fumbles with his rifle. As he narrowly avoids the sword, he puts himself exactly where I want him.

I nail him hard with my shoulder, sending him flying backwards. The lightning rifle falls between us.

In a blink, he's already on his knees about to spring forward, and I put the barrel of my mana-pistol on his forehead.

"If you're going to leave here alive, you're going to do two things. Do you understand me?" I'm breathing hard and fast.

He looks past me, up at the sky. The same terrified, doomed expression that I saw on the others is now on his face.

I press the barrel into his forehead. "Do you understand me?" I bark at him.

He nods quickly, mumbling some form of agreement.

"Why is everyone scared of those things?"

"Things?" he says, confused.

"The birds," I yell at him. I push him backwards, getting him to focus on me. "The birds. The yigging fire birds!"

"How... How do you not know?" He's completely beside himself, like I've asked him why getting shot's a bad idea.

I don't have time for this. My head's starting to spin.

"Which way are the horses?"

He's staring up at the birds again.

I snap my fingers in front of his face.

Nothing.

I smack him. That gets his attention. "Which way to the horses?"

"That… that way," he says, pointing. Suddenly, a calm falls over him and he stares at me, studying me. "You're the guy! You're the one she's looking for. Cap —"

Blam.

I watch as his headless body falls backwards.

Peering over my shoulder, the trio's running off, screaming about the Wizard and someone killing a soldier.

I return the sword to my back and my pistol back into its holding spot in my pants. I snatch the lightning rifle off the ground, and to my surprise, it feels like home.

Running my hand along it, I can feel the pulsating hum of the energy charged up and ready to be released.

Huh, this thing looks decades old. It's got a lot of scratches and dents and several welded patches, even some rust spots.

I sling it over my shoulder and look around. There's a mob of people heading my way, and I don't want to find out why.

One of the people screams, "The Wizard is here! Get out while you can! She'll burn us all alive!"

My blood runs cold. That's the demonic woman's voice. It's the Wizard. Yig me.

There's a pounding on my memory wall like a drowning man with his last seconds of air.

Taking a deep breath, I dare to gaze upward. It's a giant disc of fire, nearly as wide as the lake bed itself. It looks like the edges of the disc are bending down, creating a dome.

Holy freaking yig cakes.

I can't swallow or move. I can't feel anything but profound dread.

Tears start streaming down my face.

Yig that! Yig that! MOVE you idiot.

Gritting my teeth, I fight with every ounce of my being.

Move! Move! Move!

episode sixteen

Crackles of lightning, gun shots, and screams are coming from everywhere. Towers of smoke are rising from all corners of the tent city.

I finally get one leg to shuffle forward, then the other one. In a few seconds, I'm running like a madman, my arms trying to keep the lightning rifle in place.

Turning the final corner, I skid to a stop. There are dead horses and human bodies everywhere.

Rubbing my forehead, I stare at the ground. The path from here's a straight line out of the lake bed. Right, I can just run like a yigging idiot.

Glancing around, I notice the top of the tavern's burning. The ring of fire's coming pretty darn close to it.

I'm about to take off when I notice something else in the sky. There are several silhouettes walking up the air like it's stairs. That's got to be the rest of the Scourge Patrol.

Without a second thought, I run for the tavern, leaping over the bodies, the lightning rifle firmly in my hands.

The main floor's deserted, as is the second. Smoke's billowing down through the upstairs floorboards and then getting sucked back up. I've probably got minutes, if that, before the third floor pays me a visit.

Smashing a window out with the butt of the rifle, I scan about, catching sight of the Scourge silhouettes.

I grab a cloth off a table, fold it a few times, and place it in the window sill. Then I kneel and brace my arm and rifle in the window. I feel like a passenger in my own body.

Running a finger along a groove on the rifle's side, I find a switch and flip it. The silver-blue lines that go from trigger to barrel tip start to glow, and the rifle starts to vibrate.

Yig, it must have discharged when I was running around. It's going to take time to power up.

A hole opens in the ring of fire ahead of the fleeing Scourge patrol.

"I'm going to miss my chance."

Frowning, my eyes darting about, I think hard.

I pull my sleeve back and place my forearm along one of the charging crystal lines. Closing my eyes, I imagine the rifle as part of me. I think of the pressure in my chest. I replay that sense of the raging river that flowed through me and out my mana-pistol that first time.

Taking a calming breath, I open my eyes. Keeping my forearm in place, my fingers holding the far end of the rifle, I instinctively flip up to two crystal lenses on the top of the rifle; one by my face and the other near the tip.

Letting out a second steadying breath, I crack a smile. "Hey guys, weren't you looking for me?" I take aim at one of the silhouettes. "Here I am."

Pulling the trigger, two bolts of lightning rip into the sky, and one of the forms blows apart. Immediately, I keel over, dropping the rifle to one side, and vomiting all over the place.

"Haha, wow," I rub my chest. "You're a yigging beast. Mother of Mercy, that's some kick."

Wiping my mouth with my sleeve, I peek out the window. Two silhouettes are standing there, in the air. "I guess I got your attention."

The far end of the ceiling caves in.

Slinging the rifle over my shoulders, I make my way down to the first floor. As I reach the tavern's doorway, the rest of the third floor crashes down into the second.

Without thinking, I take out my mana-pistol, though I feel nothing in my chest. Carefully, I poke my head out. I don't see anyone.

Do I run or do I stay? I hate this.

My gaze settles on the water trough for the horses, and my mind starts going.

Where are they? Aren't they coming after me?

Taking a deep breath and holding it, I bolt over to the trough. I toss my mana-pistol and rifle to its far side, and dive in. Making sure that I'm soaked to the bone, I climb out and pick up my weapons.

If things are going to get hot, at least I've got the most basic protection. I freeze for a moment, wondering if water does anything for magical fire. I almost slap myself; now's not the time.

Looking up, I notice that the hole's gone, as are the silhouettes. That flaming ring of death's looking a lot closer.

"If you're burning all of this to get to me, I'll admit, I'm impressed."

I wince as a spark of pain runs through my head. I swear the demonic voice just got louder.

Bending down to rob a dead man of his gloves, I put them on. If things are going to heat up, I don't want to drop the rifle or a sword.

I watch as the fire dome descends low enough to consume the top floor of the bar. Flaming birds start breaking away, attacking everything.

Spinning around, I see that the edge of the dome

hasn't hit the ground yet. I set the rifle to start charging and bolt.

Leaping over dead bodies and darting past the final, feuding, few citizens of the tent city, I can feel my clothes drying out with each step.

What nightmare reality is this?

Where are you?

I trip and crash to the ground. What the yig was that? Glancing around in a panic, I can't see anything.

You're close, I can feel it. Where though, weslek? You're making a believer out of me. If it weren't for this distraction, I'd come and get you myself.

It's the demonic woman's voice. Swallowing hard, I get back up and run. My feet are hurting, and my ribs are screaming. I guess whatever the pendant did is gone.

I have no room for any thought other than run. Run. Run. Run.

The wall has only got another five feet to come down, but it's only ten yards away. I can make it.

The heat is unbelievable, and I'm getting dizzy. The wind is rushing, burning my face. My legs feel like I'm running through thick mud. My shoulders and arms are going numb.

There you are, says the demonic voice.

Below the descending fire wall, I see two soldiers lying down.

"Eat this," I yell, firing the charged rifle in mid-stride.

As the lightning flashes, I'm sent spinning in the air like a rag doll.

I land with a horrible crunch. Coughing out blood, I push myself back up and grab the strap of the rifle. Stumbling forward, it feels like the world's shifting beneath my feet.

Five yards to go, and four feet before the fire dome's sealed.

My eyes are nearly entirely shut; the heat and light's almost too much to bear.

Reaching down deep into the last reserves of my soul, I run and dive forward.

I black out before I land, the buzzing in my head overwhelming me.

episode seventeen

I close the door and stare down at my hand on the silver handle, confused and disoriented. The door's made of a rich, dark-red wood. It has shimmering rivers of gold that move from the wall-side and pool in an ornate sun in the center.

Touching one of the rivers, I marvel at how it ripples in response, yet I feel nothing.

Stepping back, I stare at the details of the sun, and my eyes go wide as I recognize it. "This is the symbol of Banareal."

"Where did you think you were?" asks a spine-chilling female voice from behind me. It's strangely familiar and kicks my heart into a panic.

I push my shoulders back and scavenge my thoughts for any idea of what I'm doing or who she is.

"Lieutenant, the right hand of the High Acolyte has asked you a question. Now, turn around." As menacing as the voice is, there's a playful undertone to it.

I glance downward. I'm wearing a decorated military uniform, a spiral of medals over my heart. On my hip is a pistol in a holster.

Raising my chin, I put on a fake smile and comply.

The chamber is huge and various shades of white, with a painted ceiling thirty feet high. Giant bookcases, full to capacity, line a side wall. The far wall is a massive window, with a view of the setting sun and the undercity far below.

On opposite sides of the room are two raised platforms. One has a huge bed and simple looking wardrobe. The other, facing the bookcases, has a U-shaped desk with papers hovering in the air around it.

There's a dark-grey-robed acolyte in the middle of the room, floating there. My heart skips a beat as I recognize the red lining and unique details of the acolyte's robes.

My hand moves towards my pistol before it stops. She was trying to kill me, wasn't she? I rub the middle of my forehead.

With a flick of her hands, the robes peel off as if they were alive and stand behind her, a ghost without a soul.

The woman has a striking, heart-shaped face. Her blond hair contrasts her dark skin and green eyes. Her gaze goes right through me and lightens my soul.

A calming sigh escapes me. "I'm okay. I... I have a

lot on my mind." I sweep the room again with my eyes, confirming there's no one else present.

"You're—" I immediately lower my gaze as I realize she's immodestly dressed.

"Really?" she says with a laugh, her voice normal and warm. "Are you sure you're feeling okay? I didn't think you even noticed things like this."

Never felt anxiety over something like this. Weird.

I watch as her bare feet make their way over to a simple-looking wardrobe.

She whispers to it, and its doors creak open. With a rush of wind, an unbelievable parade of clothes spill into the room and dance gently in the air around her.

Plucking what she wants, she then whispers again, and all the clothes vanish into the too small wardrobe.

She walks over to the edge of her bed and gets dressed.

"I know you don't ever stare, but you know you can't hide anything from me." She stands up, and I look at her. Her eyes are trying to hide her own pain. "You just got back from another outing with his Oneness, didn't you? That must be the fifth in two weeks? How many people does he need to burn and slaughter before he realizes he's the problem?"

Without thinking, I shrug, a chill running down my spine. It's strange. I can't find her name, but I feel the gravity of her spirit, and I know I've never heard her talk this way before. My gut also tells me that it's dangerous to speak this way.

Wiping my face, I swallow and look at her half-smile. "It's the sixth outing. I was told you wanted to see me. Though, I heard on my way that you were supposed to be meeting with his Oneness now."

She quickly glances away, her face twitching. Scratching the side of her nose, she puts on a shrewd politician's smile.

"It's later. Did you witness his new weapon?" she asks, tugging on the cuffs of her blouse and short, blue jacket. She shakes her head and pulls her long hair out from under the collar. Smoothing the top of her dark-blue skirt, she nods to herself, satisfied.

Even dressed like one of the aristocracy, she radiates power and determination. Her smile is infectious.

Licking my lips, I take a step forward. "The new flaming birds are... horrific. He had them encircle a village and then, as people tried to escape, had them transform into a dome of fire. He..." My throat tightens, and my eyes well up. "He brought the roof of the dome lower and lower until there was nothing."

Making fists of my trembling hands, I continue. "I thought he was simply going to use it to scare them, but… he keeps using it. And with every outing, it's worse. I don't even believe he asked them anything about rebels; he just burned them all. Even his allies and those devoted to the cause." I furrow my brow. "It's…" I straighten my jacket. "It's not how things have ever been, and I'm afraid of where they are going."

She waves at one of the bookshelves, and the books swing forward together like a door. Behind them is a suite of bottles and glasses that come forward.

I raise an eyebrow. "Feeling bold? That's some serious contraband."

"Is that a threat or observation?" she asks, with a wry smile.

She takes a bottle of green liquid and opens it. "I had a disturbing experience myself… it's why I needed to see you." She looks at me over her shoulder, her gaze piercing right through me.

Tilting my head to the side, I give her a narrow-eyed stare. "Are you at the edge of my thoughts?"

Her expression flashes to embarrassment. "I'm sorry. I shouldn't have done that. I'm just…" She looks away, and I see her face tighten, her jaw slide forward.

"You know you can always trust me," I tell her, moving to stand by her side.

She flashes me another smile and hands me a drink.

"I know," she says, staring into her glass. "Communal crime." She tinks her glass against mine. "It's actually an elixir, blocks *him* out."

My face falls.

"He's just a man... just a man. A powerful, paranoid, crazed man with limits and weaknesses." Her words are laced with anxiety and fear, dusted with courage.

She takes a sip.

I do, too.

She laughs at the sight of me drinking and rubs the edge of her nose with her glass hand. "I thought it was going to be more of a battle to get you to drink with me."

A flash of images hit me. I take a deep breath, regaining my balance. Looking at her now, she looks different. I see a sister, a friend, and more. It's like looking into a mirror that shows my other half.

I brush the back of my hand along her cheek. "I have never seen you like this. The last time you were even close was that day you killed an acolyte with a rock. We were only eight, and you saved us."

She refills her glass. "He was going to kill us because we were poor. What kind of reason is that? Filth polluting a district that would be demolished in its entirety, only to rise again as the most expensive part of the undercity."

"I think about it a lot lately," I say. There's no memory to fit, but I feel the emotion in my chest.

She points a finger of her glass hand at me, a sorrowful smile crossing her face. "The bullet rock... I was certain they were going to burn us for fighting back, but instead his Oneness conscripted us, and here we are." She lifts her drink, her eyes haunted. "And now, I look at him like that acolyte, except he sees everyone as the poor."

"What's going on?" I ask, glancing over my shoulder at the door. I notice that I have a lightning rifle slung on my back.

She puts her drink down on the shelf and stares deeply into my eyes.

"You know I would give my life for you," I say, the words flowing out without thought. The feeling inside is strange and foreign.

She draws a slow, deep breath. "A few days ago, I was sent into the undercity to root out the seeds of the rebellion. You know they arrested the last High Acolyte on charges of treason, don't you?"

I nod, taking another sip of my drink.

"His Oneness asked me personally to go, right in front of the new High Acolyte. I could tell he was bothered by it." She chokes up and glances up at the ceiling.

"His Oneness," she continued, "went on about my ruthless devotion and how I would wipe out the rumors and rebellion. How the High Acolyte should watch me. I thought... I thought I was doing the right thing."

"And you were," I say, concern spreading across my face.

Her pupils flash green, and the robes come to life and float over. She reaches into a pocket and pulls out a dark-red orb.

I'm about to ask what it is, when I'm hit with the sense that I've seen it before. My eyes dart back and forth between the robe and the orb. I can't place it. "What is that?"

"It's a sphere of knowledge, a tool of the rebellion. I saw my first one a year and a half ago. The first ones were crude things, storing a phrase or thought and draining the messenger of a good portion of their life essence."

She turned the orb in her hands. "This is the most advanced one I've ever heard of, never mind seen. It's been rebuilt and improved several times. Yesterday I locked myself in here and took it completely apart."

Her expression melts into one of tearful anguish. "I discovered it stores a piece of each person who has used it. It's why we've been able to kill the leaders of the rebellion, and yet it continues without skipping a beat. His Oneness has no idea. He hasn't believed any reports about these things, because no one has ever had a working one before."

My head shakes back and forth. "I don't understand. How could this red ball wound you so much? You are an anchor of conviction, a model of the devoted. Our cause is noble and righteous."

"But our cause isn't," she blurts out.

My blood runs cold. "What are you saying?"

She covers face with her hands for a moment before turning them into fists and shaking them violently. "I ended the rebellion. I... I went down there, and I was as thorough as I've ever been. I found the new leaders as they got together for their first meeting, and I killed them. I killed all the people who led me to them." She's staring at the floor, and I see tears roll down her face for the first time in her life.

"You did your job, why aren't you happy?" I ask.

"Because they're right. I caught the orb before it could go on and ripped the mind of the leader who had just used it. With that, and a day to myself, I broke the orb's protections and accessed everything on it."

"You ripped a mind? Only a wizard or apprentice can do that," I say, taking a step back.

She gives me a cold, hard stare.

My head's shaking back and forth. "The rumor that he's been training you to take over for him when he eventually passes, it's true?"

She stares up at the ceiling, swallowing her emotions. "He started training me two months ago. He bound me to silence. You know I couldn't tell you; even a whisper would have been picked up the next time I was with him."

"Yeah…" I say, wounded.

Picking up her glass, she fills it and drinks it in one shot. "It's why I know everything from the orb is true. The rebels are right. He's building a weapon to devastate magic on an enormous scale."

I drop but catch my glass.

"The fire dome was just a start, almost a distraction. He wants to shatter the peace with the other wizards, and he believes that the divine will protect his use of magic. He's convinced they're vermin, a disease on civilization."

She puts her drink down as her cheeks go flush. "All of the memories and feelings of all the people who have held that orb, they're part of me. I can't block them out."

I stare at my glass. "Are you certain? Maybe these are just rebel lies?"

She taps the side of her head vigorously. "I've seen it. I've seen it through the eyes of those that have seen it. And I... I went to one of the new weapons levels of the palace yesterday afternoon."

"You what?"

"The information was right. He really is mad. The Wizard of Banareal wants the world to bow before him or burn, and I don't think he cares which at the end of the day."

My heart's racing. "Surely there are others," I say, taking her hand.

"There aren't!" She pulls away and runs her fingers through her hair. "My efficiency was absolute. There's no one else. I stopped the orb from reaching the next person in the chain, and then I killed that person." She steels herself. "We are going to have to stop him. We need to be that rebellion. Like two eight-year-olds against an acolyte."

Suddenly the door bursts open.

episode eighteen

The High Acolyte, in his black robes that have a life of their own, floats into the room. A dozen Scourge soldiers with lightning rifles swarm in after him.

She pulls me close and stuffs the orb in my hand, whispering something that slips under my memories. I can't move.

As she pulls the pistol from my holster, I hear her voice in my head apologizing. She then shoots herself.

Finally able to move, I stuff the orb into my jacket and stare at her limp body. My mind is numb. Blood's dripping off my face.

The High Acolyte comes up beside me, his wraith-like form swaying back and forth.

Out of the corner of my eye, I see the Scourge soldiers, some of whom were under my command earlier in the day, with their weapons at the ready.

"Lieutenant, you should know that minutes ago, his Oneness declared her a traitor." The voice of the

High Acolyte makes my bones rattle.

"Oh." It's all I can muster as a response. I know better than to ask why or seek evidence. I also know I need to sail through these next few moments skillfully if I don't want to end up dead or in prison.

The High Acolyte floats in front of me, the haunting blackness of his hood forcing me to stare at it. "Now the question is, why did she kill herself? And what did she say to you? Neither I, nor even his Oneness, could feel either of your minds for a time."

I tilt my head away from him as I feel a chill in my mind. "It is most likely my grief that I feel at the edge of my thoughts, as it is illegal for any save his Oneness to touch an officer's mind."

He raises a hand. "That has changed. His Oneness now allows the High Acolyte to do so as well. But... given we've known each other for quite some time, I apologize. It was, if nothing else, presumptuous, if not rude."

Wiping the blood off with my hand and flicking it to the ground, I try to channel the grief rising up in me to anger. I glare at him. "She said she was overcome with guilt for killing the leaders of the rebellion. She ripped one of their minds, and it infected her."

He pushes around at the edges of my thoughts. I can feel his frustration, the drink's effects likely holding him at bay. "That is a lie."

"Who am I to question the High Acolyte? But here we are, and that is what she said."

He sways back and forth in front of me, before heading for the door. "You have served his Oneness well." He pauses, his new tone more personal. "I know she was like family to you, Lieutenant. I will inform the Grand Commander of your tragedy. Take a few days to handle the affairs you need to."

I wipe the remaining blood off my chin and cheeks. "Thank you," I force out through gritted teeth.

The room echoes with the sound of the soldiers leaving.

The door closes.

I take my coat off and throw it aside, rolling my sleeves up.

Staring at the bottles, I refill my glass and down it, twice.

Tears drip down as I gasp for air. My soul feels like it's been shattered into pieces. Gazing down at her, I fight as hard as I can, but several sobs escape.

I grab the bottle and sit down on the ground, my head leaning against the bookcase. I watch as her forearm tattoos reappear and glance at my own. Memories of how important it was to her that no one knew that secret we shared, how it told the story of our upbringing and meeting and more. Not even the

Wizard himself could detect it through her radiating passion and drive.

With a swig from the bottle, my emotional dam bursts and I sob uncontrollably. I feel alone, abandoned.

I snatch my coat off the floor and pull the orb out. Part of me wants to smash it to pieces, to scream at it. If it hadn't come into her life, she'd still be alive. But I don't. Instead, I study it, its every marking and dent. "Is there any of you in here?"

Holding the orb in one hand, I gently stroke her arm. For a while, I drink and sit there, until I'm out of tears.

"Open this for me... please?" I say to her, waving the orb. "You can't leave me like this. I need to see what you saw. I need to know you weren't betrayed or tricked. And if the Wizard's doing what you said, then I will lead the rebellion. I will kill him myself."

Silence.

I stroke her arm again and press the orb right up against my forehead.

Words escape out my mouth, the orb glows, and my mind is bombarded with the remnants of all of those before me.

episode nineteen

"Lieutenant, you are up next. Lieutenant?"

Blinking, I shake my head and focus on the young man. "Sorry, I was lost in thought. It's been a… a very long day." It's felt like an eternity since her funeral yesterday, never mind her death the day before.

The attendant is a young man, probably in his late teens, early twenties. They never last. The good ones move up the ladder; the bad ones vanish.

In front of him is a raised table with papers in piles and stones of a variety of shapes and sizes. He stares at a two-foot-wide by one-foot-high flat stone. The blue glow is reflecting off his face, making him look sickly.

Taking a deep breath, I get that sinking feeling again. A piece of me wants to drop all of this, to believe that she died confused, her mind infected. But then it's extinguished by a geyser of rage and injustice, and I'm left soaked once again in the memories and thoughts from the orb, including hers. Nothing is going to derail me. Nothing.

Gazing upwards, I stare into the cavernous darkness of the palace ceiling. The lighting in the planning wing is remarkably poor. Though it doesn't matter I suppose, given the number of safeguards and wards. Maybe this will be useful someday.

The corridor's forty feet wide, with glowing circular stones hung on the walls every five feet.

"The High Acolyte and Grand Commander are ready for you now," says the attendant, moving his hands before the large, flat stone.

I tug on my uniform's jacket, right below my neck, and clear my throat. I run a finger along my neck to my chin and realize I didn't shave. That's a first. There's no time to change that. I just need to accept there's going to be a lot of firsts.

Putting my hand up to my mouth, I'm relieved to find there's no hint of the elixir on my breath.

Closing my eyes for a moment, I find that ball of anger and anguish instead of me and crack it open. When the elixir won't hide, raw emotion will.

"Is everything okay, Lieutenant?"

The attendant coughs and points at the painted wall. He picks up a stamp and readies a piece of paper to mark that I have entered.

I offer a sharp nod and push my shoulders back. Frowning at the wall, I walk up to the painted doors, keeping an eye on the attendant for his reaction. He's waiting expectantly.

Am I being played? How does this work?

Rubbing my forehead for a moment, I think. A lot of things have been coming to me, but this... Don't think, just do.

Staring at the door handle, I reach out and, to my surprise, grab hold of it. The door then swings open, revealing the master planning room inside.

A quick glance about brings a sense of strong familiarity.

In the middle of the room is a long table decorated with wooden and stone figures, maps, and papers of all sorts.

To my left is the Grand Commander. She's in uniform, her red hair braided, a silver pistol on her hip. She's leaning away from the table, her arms folded. Behind her, seated against the wall, are a half-dozen aides writing down what she says or providing her whatever information she requests.

On the other side of the table is the High Acolyte, in a simple black, long-sleeved shirt and pants. His official robes are floating in the far corner of the room.

He's leaning on the table, his mess of curly, black hair hiding half of his bearded face. His aides are seated behind him, serving the same role as the Grand Commander's.

Behind me comes the sound of stone grinding

pebbles into dust as the door closes.

The Grand Commander raises a hand for me to wait a moment, her focus on the table.

She takes a deep breath and shakes her head. "The soonest we can hit there is in an hour, most likely two. I think we need to be careful not to create the rebellion we're hoping to crush. It's been days since we've got wind of even the soft whispers of activity."

The High Acolyte stands up and pushes on his lower back. "If we crush them properly, we won't have to worry about even the idea of rebellion, now will we?"

He turns and looks at me. "Welcome, Lieutenant." He pauses. "You seem a little rough around the edges."

I shrug.

"We read through your request for transfer earlier," he says, pointing to a pile on the table.

Keeping her arms folded, the Grand Commander stares at me. "Are you sure you want to transfer away from the field? I have to admit I was more than a little surprised, given what happened two days ago, that you want to… how did you put it?" She picks up a paper. "Wage war on those within our walls who would attempt to denigrate what we've built."

Putting my hands behind my back, I bow my head before speaking. "If I am to believe the commendations and praise I have received over the years, I have been highly effective when it comes to keeping the peace and waging war on our enemies. This rebellion, this potential insidious secret war by another wizard, it has claimed someone who meant the world to me. I will not rest until we have rooted out the cause and all those that support it." My face twitches with rage. I can feel my cheeks go flush, my jaw slides forward.

The High Acolyte studies my face, but I can feel him on the periphery of my thoughts. "So much emotion."

"What do you think?" The Grand Commander asks her colleague.

He strokes his chin and finally offers a supportive nod. "He'd be an asset, that goes without question. We don't have anyone like him on the inside."

"My thoughts exactly." The Grand Commander offers me a grin. "I have no issue with the request. Though that said," she looks at me sternly, "if I have any reason for concern, you will find yourself back out in the field."

"Of course, sir," I say, nodding.

"So, we are concluded then?" She turns to the High Acolyte.

"I suppose we are."

The Grand Commander turns to me. "Your

request is granted. However, given your state, I'd like you to take another three days' leave. Do what you must so that you can properly focus on the tasks to come."

"Thank you."

"You may go," says the High Acolyte with a dismissive wave.

I turn, and the stone door opens. As soon as I'm out of sight of the attendant, I pull out a silver flask from my pocket and take a sip.

Leaning against a wall, I let go of the anger and sorrow sweeps in to fill the void. I pound the wall. "I can't even remember her name! What's her name?"

It was no surprise that her name wasn't on any of her belongings, given how things are run. I'd have to steal a list or ask someone, and given the current state of affairs, I would be immediately flagged for suspicion.

I head for my room and change into civilian garb: a brown, long coat with matching slacks and a white shirt. Taking a leather satchel from the top of my dresser, I put the orb in along with a book and other effects.

As I head for the door, I stop and stare at the three boxes, everything that remains of her. Emotions try to consume me, but I beat them back. My face twitches with rage and I walk out.

Destiny awaits.

episode twenty

Arriving at one of the grand elevators, I'm relieved that the people I recognize are satisfied with brief smiles and small waves. No one's forcing a conversation. The rumors have spread, along with awkwardness. It's allowing me to hide my internal turmoil under the guise of grief.

The elevator doors open, and I enter along with fifty others. I move to the back and hold on to the outer railing rather than the one that runs along the ceiling.

I can't remember the last time that I stared out the glass walls of the hexagonal elevator. It's a magical experience, watching the descent to the undercity.

Glancing over my shoulder, I see everyone's facing inward, holding on to the outer or over-head railing.

There's a painful buzzing building up in the back of my mind, and I'm feeling strangely warm. I loosen the top button of my shirt and tug on it to let heat escape. The person beside me raises an eyebrow and pulls her coat tightly closed.

Staring at my reflection in the window, I feel like I'm not supposed to be here. I hear echoes at the back of my mind, telling me to get up, but I'm up.

The railings glow green, and the familiar chimes play, alerting us to the drop. I smile at the momentary shift in my weight, like every kid does when on the elevator for the first time.

As it descends to the undercity, I watch the specks become buildings, levi-cars, and finally people.

I lean my forehead against the glass. My head's a mess of questions, from why am I going to throw away a life and career to how could I have let the High Acolyte live after storming his chambers.

The thing that makes my stomach turn over and over is, what if the orb and its magic is a rebel trick designed to create traitors?

The railing glows blue, and the chimes play again. My knees bend as we decelerate; I don't even notice the heaviness.

I follow the crowd out of the elevator and into the receiving building. Soldiers are watching on the main level and the balcony. No one pays them any mind, except me.

My nervous fingers find their way into my satchel and around the orb. My heart's racing. Glancing about first, I take another swig from my flask, making sure no one sees. I can't afford to be picked up on charges of drinking in public and run the risk of having the orb discovered.

I touch my forehead expecting to find it sweaty, but it's dry. I tug on my collar again.

Clutching the orb in the satchel, I concentrate on the image of a man I met decades ago, a master craftsman.

He was one of the few free wesleks in Banareal, and he spent most of his time repairing whatever was brought to him. Like many, he had a gift for understanding how machines worked. It was by accident that I came to learn just how capable he was, and if anyone could craft the short sword that's needed, it's him. I hope he's still alive.

Walking out of the receiving building and up the steps to the street, my group thins down to a dozen, but it's still enough to distract prying eyes.

As we walk by an alley on the way to the public transit shuttles, I pluck the orb from my satchel and throw it into the alley.

I stop and pretend to read a sign, watching the orb out of the corner of my eye. I'm relieved as it arcs up and away.

I walk around for an hour, expecting a Scourge Patrol or the High Acolyte himself to show up, but no one does.

Standing in a park, eating a roll from a street vendor, I notice smoke rising from a far-off district; most likely the Grand Commander's operation is underway.

Walking about aimlessly, I find myself standing in front of a bookstore. Looking up, I recognize the sign: Owl's Nest Books. I've been here before. Looking through the shop window, a woman with short, curly, red hair waves for me to come in. I smile and walk off.

I take a gold box, about the length of an index finger, out of my satchel and flip up its cover.

Three o'clock. I've been out for a few hours now. The first part of my treachery is done, and my life's not imploded… at least not yet. I breathe a sigh of relief.

I turn onto a side-street to cross over to the next shopping district, my courage to take the next step in my plan not there yet.

Pulling up a sleeve, I stare at my arm. It feels like it's burning, but I don't see anything. I pull on my collar again. Maybe I'm losing my mind.

Taking a swig from my flask, I look up at the towering apartment buildings on either side of me.

"Oh yig," I mutter as a dot in the sky arcs down and heads straight for me. It's an orb.

"No, he has to be alive. He has to be," I yell, rushing towards it, a hand open to catch it.

As the orb hits my hand, I'm struck from behind.

My head hits the ground hard, and the world spins.

I put a hand down, ready to push myself up, but I fall back to the ground.

Everything goes black.

episode twenty-one

My head falls forward, jerking me awake. I'm being dragged.

Opening my eyes to the thinnest of slits, I flinch at the harsh brightness of the upside-down world.

The smell of burning fills my nostrils. The tent city.

Very carefully, I check out the figure on my left. A male soldier's dragging me by the upper arm, a sack over his shoulder and two rifles on his back. I've got to assume there's another soldier dragging me from the other side.

"We're far enough that the fire dome shouldn't be scrambling it as bad. Try again," says the soldier on my left.

They drop me to the ground. Keeping my eyes nearly closed, I look at the soldier on my right.

He pulls out two rectangular stones, about the length of his palms. One he holds in the air, the other he holds to his ear. "Can you hear me now?"

Hey, the soldier who I took the lightning rifle off of had those. I remember now.

He shakes the stones furiously, glaring at his colleague. "What the yig's going on over there? Bunch of kinpaks."

A wave of nausea hits me, but I remain still.

There's something familiar about the faded uniforms. The cuffs of the pants and jackets, they're threadbare. The colors are faded. These aren't cheaply made, they're vintage.

My head feels like it's going to split open as I try to figure out why I recognize them. My stomach's quivering.

"Hey, I think he's awake. Look, he's wincing," says the soldier on the left, pointing.

"Keep an eye on him," says the other soldier.

His buddy drops the sack and pulls a brown and black pistol out, pointing it at me.

"Hey! Hey, are you there?" says the soldier on the right into the rectangular stone, his other arm craned in a strange position. "Listen, I think we got the guy you were looking for. He actually made it out, nearly took us out, too. Dangerous kinpak, this one."

The soldier glares at the rectangular stone and then puts it back to his ear. "What does he look like? I don't know, he looks like a guy. The type you want to punch in the face in a bar." He glances down at me.

"He's wearing a singed vest and stuff. He had someone's lightning rifle, some weird pistol, and a pair of nasty swords."

He stares off into the distance. "Uh huh. Yeah. Sorry?"

He moves his other arm. "You're... what? What's that? Hello?"

Staring at the ground with a haunted look, the soldier on the right puts the stones away.

"What's wrong?" asks his buddy, glancing up from me over at him. "You look spooked."

"The Captain started yelling orders to protect her Oneness... something about being overrun."

"Overrun? By what?" asks the soldier on the left, his hands starting to shake.

"I... I don't know. The last thing he said was blow it."

The soldier with the pistol steps away, rubbing his face.

A wave of nausea hits me. Magic must have just failed.

There's a huge whoosh sound as the fire dome dissipates.

"Did they just set off an anti-magic bomb?"

"Or someone's used it to get at her Oneness."

The soldiers stare at each other.

I punch the soldier with the gun hard in the knee, and he drops to all fours. Following up with a solid shot to the chin, I grab him by the collar with both hands and pull him on top of me in time for his buddy to put a bullet into his friend.

Reaching over for the newly abandoned pistol beside me, I fire at the remaining soldier, but he steps out of the way.

I shove the dead guy off me and roll aside, narrowly missing being shot. I accidentally pull the trigger, but the pistol doesn't go off.

Empty.

Getting to a crouch, I throw the pistol at him, hitting him right in the face, and dive for the sack. Finding my mana-pistol, I whip around.

We've got pistols pointing right at each other, and we're both breathing heavy.

The soldier wipes the blood from his broken nose with his free hand. "I have to say, that was impressive. But it was pointless."

I furrow my brow. Why isn't he all ticked off that his buddy's dead? Are they trained psychos?

"Just so you know, you aren't getting out of here. Her Oneness knows you're here, she'll be here in minutes to get you, and then she's going to take you apart, weslek. She says you're the key to the treasures of the past."

"I'm sorry to disappoint you guys, but I already have plans," I say to him, glancing about.

"Consider them canceled." He points at my pistol. "We both know you can't fire that right now." Raising a hand with two colored rings, he smiles. "The colors change to tell me when anti-magic's in effect. I'm told you can feel it. So, no magic means no conversion of life to mana and mana to magic. So, I've got a bullet, and you've got nothing. Time to put your gun down."

I blow a blue, smoking hole clean through his chest. He drops to his knees, his face frozen in confusion.

"It doesn't work that way with us wesleks. I'd explain, but you're a bit more dead than I usually like." I watch as he falls backward.

Emptying the sack, I keep an eye on them. I'm feeling paranoid.

With the serrated swords on my back, and stealing a hip holster from one of them for my mana-pistol, I'm ready to go when it finally hits me. They're both wearing mouse pendants like me.

I take mine off and hold it up beside one of theirs. Mine looks dull, but otherwise they're identical.

Quickly, I remove their pendants and step back, my mana-pistol in hand. Wincing as the pain in my ribs returns, I immediately the pendants on my shirt, under my vest. "Do your thing, little Randmons."

Then I feel it, magic returning. Lightning rifles crackle in the distance. I shake my head. "Got to stay focused."

I salvage the two rectangular stones and study them. They've got shiny green lines and strange markings. I hold it up to my ear, but there's only the sound of rushing water.

"Hmm."

Checking I've got everything, I look around and catch a blur of action happening at the north end of the lake bed. I remember that's the direction the soldiers were looking at when talking about the Wizard, her Oneness as they called her.

I watch as several bolts of lightning flash and bodies are thrown through the air, only to land and return to the fray.

"What the? Is that oners?" I pull up the magnifying lens on the lightning rifle and get a closer look.

"Ghouls. That's a yigging insane number of ghouls." Lowering the rifle, I scan the rest of the horizon; there's nothing else going on.

Slinging the rifle over my shoulder, I wipe my face and mull over my options. If I go help the Scourge, I'm certain they'll turn on me and take me to the Wizard, who's got some nasty plans for me. But if I try to head out on my own, given my luck, those ghouls are going to find me in the dead of night.

And here I was, planning on not dying today. I guess that guy was right. My plans are canceled.

episode twenty-two

Taking the shirt off my head and wrapping it around my face, I head for the charred tent city. I'm not sure what I'm doing, but my gut says it's the thing to do, and who am I to argue?

Despite magic having returned, the fire dome's still out, and the sky's clear. Maybe the Wizard's dead.

As I descend to the floor of the lake bed, I focus on the tavern. It's completely lost the third floor, and one of the side walls has crumbled.

There's an explosion on the ridge, but I ignore it and keep going. The more they kill each other, the better.

With the rifle in hand, I make my way up to the ashy edge of where the fire dome had been.

The smell of death fills my nose. Hmm, something's not right. I take another sniff. It should be overwhelming, but instead, it's like this place burned weeks ago. Weird.

Bending down, I put my hand out over the chalky

black that blankets the entire area. It's not hot or even warm. I smear my hand along the ground and rub my fingers together. It's a mix of mana residue and soot.

"This is a bad idea. The Wizard might be able to just bring the fire birds back, and then I'm really screwed."

The buzzing spikes, reminding me that it's there and shoving me forward. "Okay! Okay." I rub the side of my head. "When I find out what the yig's wrong with me…" I grumble. "In and out, and then I head for the smoke in the west."

Standing up, my joints creak and complain.

"Shut up. You can complain all you want when I die, okay?"

I put my foot down in the black dust and remove it, studying the impression. Hmm, anyone who comes along is going to be able to find me, no problem.

"This just gets better and better."

I head straight for the tavern. It's hard to imagine the labyrinth of trails that were driving me crazy. It's all gone. Only the barest remains of people are visible.

Glancing down, I notice something odd and stop for a minute. It's an outline of a bird. I spot a number of them. It's eerie.

About fifty feet before the tavern, I glance up at the ridge. I don't see anything. It's been quiet for a while. That's not good. How long would I have before trouble shows up?

Looking back at my trail, I wonder if I should run in circles and double back, but that's going to eat too many of my precious minutes.

Turning back to look at the tavern, I find myself thinking of the Blindfold Man. "I'm here because of him, aren't I?"

Approaching the tavern carefully, I see that the second floor's gone too, never mind the third. Most of the back wall's fallen over in large chunks of mortared stone.

Stepping up to the doorway, I see it's a complete collapsed mess.

I scratch the back of my head. "What the yig's tugging at me in there?"

Rubbing my scratchy face, I shake my head. "I've come this far, let's see what it's got."

With the rifle in hand, I tour the perimeter looking for a good way in and making sure there's no one lurking.

I find a crawl space that runs from the west side towards where the bar was.

Crouching down, I give the structure a shake. It holds, but there's no way I can get in there with all my gear.

I rest the rifle against some debris, fighting with myself to let it go. Next, I take the swords off my back and put on my gloves.

The buzzing in my head kicks up. "Yig! Leave me alone! Freaking yig cakes, you suck." I give my head a whack.

Getting down on my hands and knees, I stare into the tunnel. There's some light coming in here and there, but not much.

"In and out. In and out. Now move."

The passage gets lower and tighter, forcing me on to my stomach. Twice my heart stops as I get stuck, but after a few seconds, I'm able to push through.

Taking a chance, I squeeze through an offshoot. It leads to a small clearing by the bar, shielded by a piece of the roof.

"Alright, now what?" I squint in the low light.

Pulling one of my gloves off and throwing it down, I cough as it makes a cloud.

After everything calms down, I run my hand along the floor. There's something fine and granular.

I scoop some up into my hand and hold it up to one of the beams of sunlight that are piercing through the roof.

"White... sand?" The buzzing relaxes. "This can't be it..." I run my hands carefully through the sand.

"Hey! If you're in there, come out slowly or we'll start using this place for target practice," yells someone nearby.

I stare at the wood around me. Most of it is at least singed, but I'm not willing to bet it won't light up. Never mind if their wizard survived. I need to remember not to go crawling into my own funeral pyre.

"Give me a sec, I'm stuck," I say as my hand runs over something hard. I pluck two things out of the sand and hold them up to the light. They look like gemstones, about two inches in size.

"Come out now. We're getting antsy. Those ghouls didn't leave us in a very good mood."

Stuffing the stones into a vest pocket, I put my gloves back on. "I'm coming out!"

Double-checking that my mana-pistol's still on my hip in the holster, I take a breath and think. Do I try to find another way and then come around behind them to ambush them, or do I head straight for them?

There's no way to know how many of them there are, and if they have a wizard, I'm screwed.

Hmm, I don't hear any demonic woman's voice in my head, but that doesn't mean much.

"Keep talking to us."

"I'm heading towards you."

As my head comes out of the tunnel, I see there's a soldier on either side of me, about two yards away. My rifle and swords have been tossed behind them.

The soldiers back up, their rifles trained on me.

"Toss that over and get up, really slowly."

I reach down and take my mana-pistol out of its holster and toss it at my other weapons. "You know, you guys like working in pairs too much," I reply with a smirk, hoping to get a rise out of one of them.

Looking at their uniforms, I see one's got more yellow markings. "You're the captain, I take it?"

He shrugs. "Doesn't really matter. If you move, we're going to light you up."

"Fair enough," I say as I slowly pull off my gloves and drop them to the ground. I'm exhausted. I'm certain that if I make a move on one of them, they'll have enough time to fry me before I can take them out.

My mouth's dry and my heart's pounding. The last thing I need to do is lose it.

The Captain steps away, letting his rifle hang from its shoulder strap. He pulls out two rectangular stones from a belt pouch, they look the same as what the other soldier had. "Let her Oneness know that we've got him. Side of the tavern. Yeah, okay. See you in two."

Staring at the serrated swords, an idea hits me. This is a bad idea, but I don't think I'm up for anything else.

Keeping my hands as steady as I can, I gently dust my face and sleeves. Sighing casually, I pretend to look around. "Is this going to take a while?"

"Don't you worry, they'll be here in a second," says the Captain.

Nodding, I gaze about, pure boredom plastered on my face. After a second, I glance down and frown. Shaking my head, I straighten my vest and slip my fingers into the pocket. Stretching, I toss the gemstones.

"What was that?" yells the junior soldier, glancing over his shoulder and then back at me.

The hum from the rifle's charging crystals are loud and clear to me.

"Just some dirt," I reply. "You want to present me to your wizard lady looking like crap? Come on." I scoff and shake my head. "Seriously…"

The world wobbles and I stumble, my arms jutting out to catch myself.

As the junior soldier grabs me forcefully by the shoulder to stabilize me, the Captain gets his rifle up and in my face.

"I'm okay," I say calmly, noting that the buzzing seems to be nearly gone. "It's been a long day. It's catching up with me."

The junior soldier shoves me, and they resume their previous distance—about two yards away.

A few seconds later, they glance at something over to my right and then back to me.

Narrowing my eyes, I listen. Something's approaching. It's a levi-car of some kind. The engine's a bit rough but sounds bigger than what I'm used to.

I give the junior soldier a smirk. "I was rooting for the ghouls, you know. Guess I picked the wrong team."

He motions like he's going to hit me with the butt of his rifle, but the Captain predictably calls him off.

"We've got some nasty friends; they don't like to lose," says the junior soldier, a smackable expression on his face.

Looking past him, I smile. "Funny, so do I."

A serrated blade punches right through his chest.

As the Captain turns to see who did it, I put everything I've got into kicking him in the chest.

Landing flat on his back, he doesn't have second to breathe before a woman with shoulder-length, black hair puts her other blade right through his heart.

"Like that, you kinpak?" she yells at him. She expertly pulls the blades out and wipes them on the Captain's chest.

I look at her in disbelief. "At first, I thought you might be a mirage. That really you, oner?"

She stares at me confused. "I'm not sure."

Out of the corner of my eye, I see a large levi with a flatbed pull into view. Three bandaged soldiers with slumped shoulders are in the back.

"We can take them," I say, and then I hear it: the demonic woman's voice.

Finally.

I look at oner, my eyes wide. "Never mind. She's here. You have to go. Now."

Who are you talking to? I feel something…

She puts out her hand, offering me the gemstone. I take it from her, and she disappears. The intense buzzing immediately returns.

The levi-car skids to a stop.

Standing straight up, I glance down at the serrated swords that are laying at my feet. So much for deniability.

The doors open. Out of one side comes a soldier, resting his lightning rifle on the hood of the levi.

"Where's the other one?" he yells.

I shrug. "It's just me. Come look if you like."

From the other door comes a dark-grey-robed figure. As my eyes pick up the red trim, I immediately feel anger, sorrow, and fear. I know this robe.

I've so been looking forward to seeing if it was really you, and it is. It truly is.

It's her. I stare, perplexed, as she walks over. I expect the robe to flow and move with a life of its own, but it seems stiff and leathery, more like a wounded beast than a thing of nightmares.

"So, the story of the impaled statue is true," she

says, her voice eerie and menacing. "I'd hoped it was you, particularly when my scavengers brought me this." She pulls out my short-sword. It looks dull and stone grey.

I glance at my weapons, but I don't have the energy. I'm tempted to throw the gemstone, but I have no idea what'll happen. For all I know, the oner woman was a hallucination, and I killed them.

"Get out of my head," I say through gritted teeth as I feel a presence at the edge of my mind.

"Hmm, you can sense that? Interesting," she says, amused. "I will take extra delight in pulling you apart. Part revenge, part curiosity, all of it wrapped in a vision for a new age."

With a wave of her hand, the hood slowly peels away, like animated tree bark. At the back of my mind, I know it's wrong, and that it isn't the robe of a wizard, but of an acolyte.

I'm ready to verbally hammer her, hoping to create an opportunity for me to get out of here, when I see her face.

That face.

My body goes numb.

"Ania?"

"Hello, weslek. You will die a thousand deaths at my hands—and then a thousand more."

The End of Season Two

THANK YOU
FOR READING THIS BOOK

Reviews are powerful and are more than just you sharing your important voice and opinion, they are also about telling the world that people are reading the book.

Many don't realize that without enough reviews, indie authors are excluded from important newsletters and other opportunities that could otherwise help them get the word out. So, if you have the opportunity, I would greatly appreciate your review.

Don't know how to write a review? Check out **AdamDreece.com/WriteAReview**. Where could you post it? On GoodReads.com and at your favorite online retailer are a great start!

Don't miss out on sneak peeks and news, join my newsletter at: **AdamDreece.com/newsletter**

PLAYLIST

Every now and then I get asked what albums I listened to when writing a book. Here's what I primarily listened to when writing The Wizard Killer - Season Two:

Heathens by Twenty One Pilots
Leaves' Eyes - King of Kings
Within Temptation - Hydra
Amaranthe - Maximalism
The Matrix Reloaded: The Album

Enjoy,
Adam

ABOUT THE AUTHOR

Off and on, for 25 years, Adam wrote short stories enjoyed by his friends and family. Regularly, his career in technology took precedence over writing, so he set aside his dream of one day, maybe, becoming an author.

After a life-changing event, Adam decided to make more changes in his life, including never missing a night of reading stories to his kids again because of work, and becoming an author.

He then wrote a personal memoir (yet unpublished) as every story he tried to write became the story of his life. With that out of the way, he returned to fiction, and with a nudge from his daughter, wrote Along Came a Wolf and created The Yellow Hoods series.

He lives in Calgary, Alberta, Canada with his awesome wife and amazing kids.

Adam blogs about writing and what he's up to at **AdamDreece.com.**

He is on Twitter **@AdamDreece** and Instagram **@AdamDreece.**

And lastly, feel free to email him at **Adam.Dreece@ADZOPublishing.com**

ADAM DREECE BOOKS

The Man of Cloud 9
ISBN: 9780-994818-430

Tilruna (Season #1)
ISBN: 9781-988746-050

The Wizard Killer, #1-3: 978-0-9948184-5-4,
978-1-988746-01-2, 978-1-988746-03-6

"Harry Potter meets Die Hard"
–M. Bybee, WereBook.org

"Madmax meets Lord of the Rings"
–Goodreads.com

A world once at the height of magical technology and social order has collapsed. How and why are the least of the wizard killer's worries.

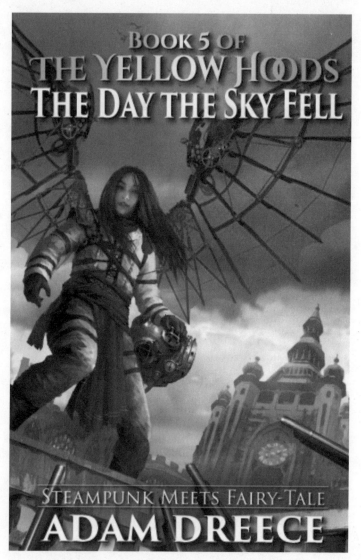

BOOK 5 OF
THE YELLOW HOODS
THE DAY THE SKY FELL

STEAMPUNK MEETS FAIRY-TALE
ADAM DREECE

An amazing steampunk meets fairy tale adventure
series for those 9-15 years old and adults alike.